Life's Bye-Ways, and What I Found in Them

SALZWASSER
VERLAG

A. Fergusson

Life's Bye-Ways, and What I Found in Them

Reprint of the original, first published in 1863.

1st Edition 2022 | ISBN: 978-3-37500-110-0

Verlag (Publisher): Salzwasser Verlag GmbH, Zeilweg 44, 60439 Frankfurt, Deutschland
Vertretungsberechtigt (Authorized to represent): E. Roepke, Zeilweg 44, 60439 Frankfurt, Deutschland
Druck (Print): Books on Demand GmbH, In de Tarpen 42, 22848 Norderstedt, Deutschland

LIFE'S BYE-WAYS,

AND

WHAT I FOUND IN THEM,

BEING

NARRATIVES FROM REAL LIFE.

BY

A. FERGUSSON.

WITH A

PREFACE BY THE REV. C. H. SPURGEON.

"Truth is stranger than fiction."

LONDON:

1863.

"ITS NO GO — NO BROWNS"

SEE PAGE 4.

PREFACE.

A MASS of musty old rags may be seen under a glass case in the palace at Amsterdam. No Jew would make half so high a bid for the lot as he would offer for the cast-offs of a pauper. Yet the value of these relics it were difficult to calculate, for they are the hallowed memorials of the Netherlanders' patience and courage, the tokens of his triumph over the half-demon Spaniard, and the altogether demon Inquisition. Hail to you spirits gone to your rest who snatched the proud banner from the standard and made its remnants the witness of your prowess. But what have Dutch, and Spaniards, and moth-eaten flags to do with these Stories of "Life's Bye-Ways?" Well—the connection is not to be found in the fact that these sketches tell of rags and troops whose tatters are the banners of their clan; but we claim a comparison, because they are the records of moral conflicts, and the relics saved from spiritual contests. You will like these fragments none the less, O most enlightened friend, because they smell of powder, and bear evidence of having seen the thick of battle, where blood, and fire, and vapour of smoke, or other stern and unfastidious influences have dyed them through and through. Soldiers do not wash the stains from their standards, or mend the shot-holes, but they hang up the old flags just as they come from the dust of the battle. Refinement may suggest polished and elegant language, but fine phrases would be out of place in this record of a rough hand-to-hand struggle. Delicate silks and snow-white muslins are to be flaunted in the pageant of a tournament; lily hands and perfumed locks belong to carpet-knights, but the rough jerkin, and the bespattered gabardine are the insignia of real men-at-arms.

MR. FERGUSSON has not disdained to be the patron of the Pariah, and the tutor of the thief. He is one of those who are willing to thrust down their arms up to the very elbows in the mire that they may rescue the fallen from the slough of depravity and despond. He has met with strange adventures in queer corners, and he does well to inform us of them, that we may sympathise the better with God's workers, and pray the more earnestly for the degraded ones among whom they labour. What marvellous things the moon sees! What tragedies and comedies are witnessed by the stars when they peer between the tiles which but half cover the garret of poverty! The world is growing very common-place to some people; the days of stirring incident and romantic enterprise dawn not upon their jaded souls; they blame their stars for their *ennui*, and scold the dull age because it gives no scope for their energies, and offers no stimulus to their mental powers. Alas ye little men, it is indeed a dwarfish age and ye make it so! But when or where was there a glorious era for a lazy man? Who makes discoveries while lolling on his couch? How can surprises happen to those who cross not their own threshold? There are few adventures in a life spent in luxury, and romantic incident never intrudes itself into the serenity of pompous respectability. You may lounge in drawing rooms, and dally in parlours for half a century, and never get so much as a peep at the glorious drama which is being enacted on the stage of this year of grace, 1863; the place for sight-seeing is in the pit of hard work among the toiling crowd, up in the gallery of crime where thieves do congregate, or away there in the solitary boxes where sickness and penury moan to each other. If we would take a walk in the "guilt gardens" of our huge city, and stoop over the young plants, we should see that our moral *fauna* has specimens as rare as any period can offer. Read the annals of the slums, and you will never complain of the tameness of current history. The courts, alleys, and crowded houses of London, contain unwritten novels, far more healthy in matter, and not less thrilling than the sensation rubbish which robs so many of their time. Come off from the gravel path of respectable society into the middle of the road with the struggling street-trader, or tarry awhile under the hedge with the gipsy or the tramp, and you shall hear a tale, at the rehearsal of which both your ears will tingle. Ladies and gentlemen, the age of chivalry was all mere milk and water compared with the rich cream of interest which this era of philanthropy puts in your way.

Improbable as these stories seem, the author has penned them just as they occurred to him. His quick eye and smart description doubtless bring out more of the colour of an event than a less sensitive observer might have noticed, but we cannot wonder at this when we remember that he feels an almost paternal interest in the lives which he pourtrays.

As no one ever thinks of reading a preface, it does not concern me much when I add that I have nothing more to say but that I wish this book a good sale, that it may be the leader of a brilliant succession of interesting and racy volumes, and that it may lead many to care for those who perish in the open streets beneath the pitiless pelting of the storm, of cold and hunger and broken hearts, or what is worse, of ignorance, disease, and the soul-withering blast of sin.

C. H. Spurgeon

ONE OF
LIFE'S BYE-WAYS,
AND
WHAT I PICKED UP IN IT.

CHAPTER I.

I CAME to reside in London nine years ago. On my arrival my feelings were those of a traveller who has reached a foreign land, about which he has read, and from his book knows well. All former memories and notions were now to be submitted for confirmation or rejection to the test of actual investigation. Like the traveller, I, too, had my darling schemes and my favourite haunts. Among the former were no dreams of the mayoralty, nor the erection of a merchant prince's throne. Among the latter I did not include the fairy scenes of our picture galleries, crystal palaces, or public gardens. My tastes have a different bias. Dearer to me than all these are the Ragged Refuge with its drab hues, and the Sunday School with its chastened bustle. The dearest associations of my heart were formed amid such scenes; my first public entry among men was there; the dust of the Sunday School soiled my first coat. For twenty years the Sabbath sun has gone down upon me either in the Night Refuge or among the cherry cheeks and shining eyes of the Sunday School. The reader, at this moment, may have little difficulty in guessing my whereabouts on the morning or in the evening of any Sabbath day. Or through the week, if absent sight-seeing, ten to one I would be found in some back court, witnessing the last new dodge for bringing the dear uncombed "loons" within range of the cross; or I might be away on some common in high glee, and up to the eyes among the festivities of a Sunday School excursion. These are the joys of the old teacher—the pleasures of the man.

During my career as a Sunday School teacher, I have observed narrowly and noted carefully its effects upon the affections of the heart and the faculties of the mind; no geographer ever traced with more delight the windings of some newly-discovered river than I have the devious stream of holy influence flowing from the Sunday School among the rough scenery of our common nature. And where is such another stream? Consider the self-denial of its fishermen as they ply their vocation of catching souls. Who can reckon the value of the pearls that lie below its soft-flowing waters? Christ declares one of them worth a world! And what, my reader, can exceed in interest its historic fame? There, he that struggled till the break of day on the banks of the Jabbok with Jacob may be seen often. There, even now, heaven and earth, hell and sin, are mingled in deadly fray, and souls are lost and won.

It is my intention, in a series of humble papers, to lay before my readers some of the scenes through which I have passed on all parts of its banks in a campaign extending over twenty years.

CHAPTER II.

Being determined, before again putting on harness, to visit some of our Metropolitan Sunday Schools, and add a few facts culled on English soil to those collected in Scotland, I laid my plan of Sunday School London (one made by myself) before me, and selected my route for the evening.

Towards the heart of the City I turned my steps. I feel towards cities in this respect as I do towards men; the heart is the part that makes right or wrong in city, soul, or body. Upon its condition depends that of the extremities in each. Being accustomed to the hill country of Scotland, I had acquired the habit of walking long distances without much fatigue. I felt a pleasure, therefore, in my first plunge into the populous wilderness of London, and in roaming, a free agent and unknown, over its awful area of streets, with the prospect of a rest in a Sunday School at my journey's close. It was a dull November day, at the close of the afternoon, I took the road. I remember it well. The fog hung in the air like a huge web of gray muslin—as thick, but not so clean. The streets were greasy and noisy; 'bus and cabmen howling and swearing at each other, and hugging the curb-stone as ships do the land in a squall; little link boys, with the speed of spirits, were darting through the gloom like minnows in a Highland stream, and possessing all the mimickry of the mocking-bird. Teasing was all this to an old Londoner, but amusing, confusing, and suggestive to the mind of a greenhorn like myself, and forming for the first time, as I that night was, my first acquaintance with a genuine London fog. I shall not soon forget the impression made on my mind when my reverie was disturbed by one of these little fellows coming up to me and waving his blazing link under my very nose, fluttering in rags, in that cold night, his locks uncombed, and under them a face resembling dirty chalk. Up from that face gleamed two eyes. I remember these eyes to this day. He left his photograph on my heart. I tried to look down into his soul through these eyes, but the air of stupidity visible in mine, I suppose, settled the question, for, as his mates shouted, "It's no go—no browns," he disappeared in the darkness. Poor little soul; I'll never see thee more. May Jesus seek and find thee; there's no stupidity in His eyes when He looks into a soul, and, instead of browns, you'll get gold tried in the fire; then, my little fellow, we will meet where link and fog are no more. You dream not of what you have done. You have wedded one soul at least, for life, to your unfortunate class. As the fiery cross roused the clans of my forefathers, and led them among mountain and valley to foray and fray, so your fiery link pointed me and all men caring for you, to the scenes and the class, where, and in which, in our large cities, the battle of the Cross is to be fought even where you are born in thousands, first ruined and then starved.

My reflections were soon disturbed by the noise around me. A wiser and a sadder man, I moved towards my destination. I arrived at one of those naked spaces, flanked on all sides by low ranges of dingy houses, met with occasionally in the very heart of London. The walls of long departed dwellings intersected it in all directions. In one of the sides of this deserted plot, by a gradual descent you approached five or six dry arches filled with oyster-shells, &c., evidently the cellars of once existing houses, but now the haunt of the thief and the prostitute. Where is the ear that could listen to the sad tales these mouldering bricks could tell were they to become vocal, as one day they will, when—

> "The blast of the trumpet, so loud and so shrill,
> Will shortly re-echo o'er ocean and hill."

Then at least, will every tub stand on its own bottom, and the saddle be put on the right horse. Looking northward as far as the eye can see extends one of those narrow streets inhabited in the days of Charles I. by merchants and the middle classes, now the abode of disease, dirt, and crime; nay, the story runs, that treason and murder have done work there, and from its sombre courts there have been sent forth victims for hangman and headsman. At this very hour, entering it, your hand moves intuitively to your watch and your purse, and your eye becomes wide-awake. Along the east side of the plot runs a line of low built houses, and in the centre stands one a little higher than the rest, having a lamp which throws a sickly ray on a battered door-way, around which is gathered a ragged, brawling multitude, clamorous for admission. This is the Ragged Sunday School I am in search of.

CHAPTER III.

THE door opens, a whoop and whistle, and up stairs they rush. I follow, quite absorbed in the scene. A gentleman, one of the teachers, seeing me a stranger, whispered in my ear, "Mind your pockets, sir, you're among some of the biggest villains in London." Seeing me astonished, he added, "Why, sir, sometimes we have had our handkerchiefs returned to us at the end of the lessons, with this remark,—'Here it is sir; I couldn't take your wipe to-night, your lesson went too deep!'" With such a scene before me, the fog around me, and that whisper in my ear, I felt like a man that dreamed.

Hark! the bell rings; each teacher finds a place, and two hundred villains are distributed in classes, as by a stroke of magic. Such a sight! Rogues, over whose gray hairs forty summers had come and gone, and little thieves between, scarcely a span long. All is still. Every eye turns towards a deal table, at which stands one of the finest specimens of England's sons. Above the middle stature, broad-chested, and strong limbed, open of countenance, with lofty forehead, and clenched lips, indicating immense firmness, yet all dimpled with smiles, such as men acquire by looking often into the Gospel. When he frowned, not a feature was left out; when he laughed, he laughed with all his face. Such is the stuff heroes are made of. This is the regular superintendent, who, out of love to his Lord and to their souls, has striven to lead them to Christ. He gently slaps his hands, all are on their feet, and over the scene rises the hymn—

"There is a fountain filled with blood,
Drawn from Immanuel's veins,
And sinners plunged beneath that flood
Lose all their guilty stains."

Then arose a burst of sacred music, a heart in every bar of it. Never to my dying day shall I forget that strain, or cease to remember that choir—every chorister a thief. How strange! What but the Gospel could group and keep them together? Where, but on the floor of a Ragged School could they be met in safety? I wept for joy I had lived to see the day. Then came a few words of simple prayer, in which that Ragged Sunday School was held up to the bleeding Lamb—nay, he seemed as if he would lead his charge through the rent veil of the Redeemer's flesh into the very arms of the Majesty on high. The school is now open; the hum of teaching fills the building. I wandered from class to class; one particularly took my attention, it was taught by a young lady. I sat down within ear-shot, looked and listened. There were four old men, three young men, and six lads. All in rags, one without a coat and gray headed; he wept bitterly, but silently, as Jesus, through her lips, besought him to be reconciled. Each bore the marks of an out-door lodger, and nearly all had been cropped at the expense of the country. From these skeletons and rags a thousand struggles looked down upon you. How earnestly did the souls of these miserable men look through their eyes as their teacher led round God's scape-goat among them and implored them to lay all their ills on its devoted head! But the bell rings, the benediction is pronounced, and all is over. The school disappears in the streets. A few linger behind, imploring some boon from the superintendent. Curiosity drew me to the spot. Two of the petitioners were members of the young lady's class, beside which

I sat during the evening—Tom by name, and a companion. They are imploring a night's lodging beside the stove. Tom looks every way eligible; he is tattered and torn, and has been roughing it among the dry arches, and suffers from cold, and a species of ague imparts a tremor to his limbs. The case roused the mercy and the firmness of the superintendent. The night accommodation is small, and the means for maintaining it is smaller still. A firm, but kindly refusal met the prayer of Tom. Turning his manly face full on that of our friend, he said, "Sir, it's my disease that makes me ask shelter; I do not want bread, only house-room." This did it; it was a stroke among the heart-strings of this man of God; he relaxed into a smile, saying—"Well, Tom, I can't give you a bed or a rug, but you may sit by the stove with the night-watch." All present rejoiced; our sufferer bowed and crept to the fire, and a grace was put upon the whole by his companion being sent after him to keep him company.

I left for my home, pondering what these things meant. The whole scene floated in my mind; the ragged sprite, with his flaming link, and that ragged man imploring for lodgings, passed hither and thither through it like visions in a dream. One I had lost for ever; to the other I determined to cling, and out of him drag his life's story. In a few days an incident occurred which gratified my heart's wish to the full. From excessive labour in the class-room, I had been spitting blood previous to my coming to London, and was compelled to desist from all work requiring the exercise of speech. Unwilling to remain idle for the time specified by the doctor, I resolved, before returning to professional labour again, to acquire a knowledge of practical book-keeping. Having mentioned this to a friend, he suggested my taking care of a few of his books at his office as the best way of attaining my object. I accordingly entered his office for this purpose. It was while so employed I had the pleasure of meeting Tom. The managing clerk asked me in the course of the week to look out for a youth, who, for a trifle would distribute hand-bills and pull a truck. My whole soul turned to Tom. I rejoiced in spirit, for my heart's desire was to lift a fallen brother, and vindicate, to that large firm at least, the utility as a nursery of the dear Sunday School. I trembled for the result. Tom was to me a stranger; what was he? whence came he? Would he stand? would he fall in the hour of trust? Would he help himself, and honour the Sunday School? Or would he fall in an evil hour, injure himself, disgrace the cause, and pluck my feathers? Full of doubts and fears, I unbosomed myself to the superintendent—told my errand. He gave him a good character, and quite approved of my choice. After earnestly entreating him to tell Tom to put his best foot foremost, and pay scrupulous attention to his toilet, to meet me to-morrow at ten in the warehouse, I left him and returned to my desk.

I waited anxiously for the morrow. I was in my place; the hour appointed came, and Tom arrived. Oh dear! oh dear! would that all the Sunday School teachers in London had been present! How the little fat clerk did stare, as in silence his sharp eye darted through and through that poor fellow, rags and all; then, with a glare of astonishment he looked at me, and back again at the object of my affections. I felt as when a young lady for the first time introduces her lover to papa and waits the issue. I blushed all over. Tom was asked to step out; I wished I had been asked to follow him. The glass door was shut.

"Sir," said the clerk, "are you aware what you have done?"

"Quite," I replied.

"There is much property lying about here, do you take the responsibility?"

"I do."

"I will look to YOU for all; I will ignore HIM."

"Do so," I retorted. Tom was engaged. A few weeks justified my choice.

CHAPTER IV.

BEING required to collect the money over one of the traveller's walks in the vicinity of London one day, it was found necessary, in order to save time, that I should have one of the men in the warehouse to assist me. I selected Tom, of course. We had a good day's work before us, and I was determined it should not close without Tom unfolding himself to me. After all our business was over, and preparations made for returning, I proposed walking in preference to riding; the day was clear and cold, but bracing, and we set out with vigour. Having cleared the village, I proposed some refreshment, and that it should be enjoyed under the hedge. No sooner said than done. Tom cleared a spot, and did it so well, I remarked, "This is not the first time you have dined under a hedge." He looked up at me somewhat confused, as if at a loss to know in what light I would view his past career if I knew it. He could have asked me—judging by his looks—If I let you into the secret, will you despise me, or pity me? My manner set him at rest, and, after asking a blessing, our simple repast proceeded. I looked Tom in the face, and said, "You seem very happy to-day; what's the cause?"

"I am so, I feel it all over me; but, sir, the simplicity of your question makes me smile." Here I looked at him; an unnatural brightness appeared in his eyes, and he seemed to draw himself up from his very toes. "My present circumstances," returning my gaze, "are as new to me as a steamship once was to a New Zealander; for the last eight years of my life, one happy day has never dawned on ME."

He seemed agitated; past memories gathered round

him like angry bees, and each, as it passed, touched him with its sting. I had pulled the right string. I, in my turn, was moved. I felt for Tom, for I loved him. I could play no longer, so I asked him to tell me of some of his struggles.

"Sir," said he, "will anything in a porter's life interest YOU?"

"Tom, everything in the life of a soul interests Jesus, your God and mine, and therefore is interesting to a believer."

What follows fell from his lips, and with that I will close this paper:—

"Well, sir, I was born in Glasgow some eighteen years ago. I am a soldier's son; disease abroad killed my father, and the cholera took away my mother. In one year my three sisters and I were made orphans, without a penny and scarcely a friend. My sisters found employment in the neighbourhood where we lived. I went to live with an uncle—a man without a heart. Oh, sir, he was ill, ill to me! After a few years, I saddened and sickened under his care, and at last ran away. With a companion, Charlie Brunton, I resolved to visit England. We set out, meeting our expenses by working from town to town. After six months, we found ourselves within fifty miles of London. Here I separated from Charlie who found regular employment, and I did not. On the day we parted we spent the afternoon and evening together, and separated at midnight, under a tree, in silence. 'Ah!

Charlie, before you and I meet again,' I said, 'we'll know both sides of the shilling.' Our arms were round each other; we stood speechless, and tore ourselves asunder. So ragged and woe-begone was I now that I was refused work. As I passed along the road, people stared and whispered; I felt I was suspected. Worst of all, sir, I was reduced from working and travelling to begging and travelling. My spirits, like lead, sank to the bottom of my heart. Well do I remember sitting under a hedge to eat the crust I had not earned, calling upon death to finish the ball. I knew enough of my Bible to believe suicide was sin, and that the rope and the river were not always the shortest cuts to happiness. My conscience would not let me murder myself; and, at that time, to me the Cross of Christ was unknown. I was pained at the heart, and I seemed to move in thick darkness. I was in despair, with only courage and reason enough left to finish the twelve miles between me and London. After a sleepless night, without one bit of cheer, one ray of hope, I took the road, believing that in the evening body and soul would finish their acquaintance on the pavement of the city. I arrived late in the evening at the west end of Oxford Street, and spent the night out of doors. I was forced to beg, so as to get a crust and a few coppers, and was able to pay threepence for a night's lodging in one of our cheap lodging-houses. May God keep me, sir, out of these dens all the rest of my life. They are worse than hells, these places—they would make devils worse than they are. Men and women lying all of a heap, drinking, swearing, and snoring in all directions; two or three tallow candles stuck in bottles, at intervals, round the room; and the walls glittering with sweat. My circumstances were now dreadful. I saw I MUST become a thief, if I remained there and have any peace. Sir, I have fallen into many sins in my time, but I am not a thief—never was." Here his manner and aspect commanded the deepest respect and almost instant belief. "Such an assembly met there one night, that I rose from the fire and walked out; the street, sir, was heaven to it. I stayed out all night and caught cold, and was seized again with ague. I thought I must surely die. In this condition I crawled down to London Bridge; I sat and trembled in a corner; I asked nothing; the crowd passed on. Towards five in the afternoon a gentleman turned aside, asked me a few questions, and gave me a shilling. He took out his card, and wrote the address of the school you found me in on the back of it. There I was received, and sheltered for a day or two. I gradually got better, and took to street-work again, and was able to earn a little—enough to keep me in bread and humble lodgings. That gentleman's card let daylight in upon me. I now became a regular attender in Miss L———'s Sunday class, and much good I have gotten there. The sour feelings towards men, and the harsh ones towards God's providence, which sprang up in me during my trials, wore away. I felt happier, somehow. It's hard to hate, sir. It makes one miserable—just like having a live coal in the palm of your hand. Yet I was no holier in my heart; all that dear lady used to tell us of Jesus did not move me; and I am sure of a Sunday night she used to drag her whole class to the very foot of the Cross. I again turned ill, was unable to work, and was once more out of a home. I was so ill that I was again compelled to ask for shelter beside the school stove; that very night you came on a visit to it. That was a night of nights to me. At that school stove I was joined by a companion—one of my Sabbath class fellows. We sat together. He was sad, and I was sadder. That night, however, he seemed softer in his mannar than he used to be, and spoke often of the Bible. We bewailed our fate; I said I was becoming hopeless and heartless; he made no reply, and I stared into the fire. At length, looking me full in the face, and laying his hand on my shoulder, he said, 'Tom, do you know I intend to put God to his word to-morrow.' I did not understand him. He said, 'Do you remember that lesson of Miss L———'s, two Sundays ago, about prayer?—I can't get it out of my mind. She said so often and so earnestly, and looked at us so, 'Lads, God hears and answers prayer.' Now, we have been nearly this whole day without bread; and she said the very ravens, when hungry, prayed, and got answers, too. Now, if

I live, Tom, I'll pray to God to-morrow. Do you pray?' I was silent; but my conscience answered—no. Here he looked earnestly up in my face, and said, 'Will you join me?' So sincere did he look, for my life I could not say no. After a little more talk we stretched ourselves upon the bench and fell asleep. The morning bell was rung: we started to our feet, washed, and were turned out for the day. When we reached the bottom of the stair the morning was raw, cold, and very dark. 'Now, Tom, do you remember your promise?' whispered a voice beside me. 'You said you would.' My companion was at my side. I demurred. '*There was no place.*' Pointing to one of the dry arches, 'This will do, Tom; come on,' he said. In he went, and I followed. Having reached the far end, he fell on his knees and burst into prayer—the exact words I can't remember, but it came from his heart. The burden of it was—*Bread, work, and pardon.*

"We both came out; we wiped our eyes—we had been crying. I had not opened my mouth; but I remember saying, as I grasped his hand, 'Now for it.' We turned down the street in the dark, and at the bottom took our stand, hungry, quiet, and waiting. We felt as if watching an experiment. Time wore on; there was nothing on the move. 'I fear,' said I, 'we are two bad uns, we are not to be heard.' My companion replied, 'Wait, Tom, wait; we cannot *command* God.' This shut my mouth: we stood in silence.

An hour had passed away. But, sir, I was wrong; God DOES hear and answer prayer. A little man, in great haste, came up to us, and said, 'Carry this bag for me to Euston Station;' and laid it down. My companion shouldered it, and I supported it from behind; we arrived at the station, he threw down two shillings and disappeared. We grasped each other's hand, we looked each other in the face, and not a word we spoke. At last I said, 'What fools are we to be running at men's heels and cringing for coppers, when God is so liberal. I'll doubt his word no more.' We spent that day by ourselves: that day Jesus tied our hearts to himself. And now, sir, this day I am here; and from that hour I have had bread, a coat, and a home. I believe it will be so to the end."

I may add, in closing, they both now adorn the doctrine of God their Saviour. Tom is at the HEAD of the warehousemen of the firm to which I introduced him. His companion is a shoemaker in a neighbouring village.

ANOTHER OF

LIFE'S BYE-WAYS,

AND

WHAT I THERE FOUND.

CHAPTER I.

OFTEN has it struck me that between the antiquary and the Christian a striking resemblance subsists. The objects of their tastes are different, and often lie wide apart. The points of resemblance between them are few, but their favourite haunts are alike—ruins, grim ruins. The one hovers like a spirit of the place, all eye, all ear, amid fallen towers, roofless churches, ivied castles, and moss-grown tomb-stones. The other lingers, all heart, amid ruined souls, in prisons, hospitals, and starving homes. Time opened up the path of the one; sin ploughed up the path of the other. Each toils to trace in the wrecks before him, the plans, the skill, the workmanship, the genius of the old masters. Those dear to the heart of the antiquary are the workers in brass, iron, and stone, in the morning of civilisation. They that are dear to the affections of the Christian are the Holy Spirit and his host of agents that have wrought and now work under his directions since the day that Adam stood weeping, broken-hearted, at the gate of Eden. To pursue the parallel a little farther, each purposes chiefly the investigation of some one particular class of objects—the works of some one particular master, the products of his pen, pencil, or chisel. To collect and preserve these, or simply to behold them, each cheerfully undergoes all the toils and troubles, perils and privations of his peculiar field of labour.

Jesus is called the "first-born among many brethren." In order to be one of them, bearing his image becomes indispensable. To bring the human soul to resemble Christ is entirely the work of the Holy Spirit. His studio is the world. One of the grand exercises of the Christian—one of the delights of his heart, is to trace the work of *his* pen, pencil, and chisel among the relics of the fall, as they lie scattered over the bosom of the living world. So vast is the range, so various the specimens, and innumerable the instances of his handy work, that to no region of the globe can the eye of the antiquary of the Cross be turned but it detects some vestiges of his skill. Yea, every man, be his language, colour, or clime what they may, must either be a sculpture on which he is at work, or a block on which hammer and chisel have never been lifted. To detect this fact, among the families of the earth, to admire his workmanship where it exists, to deplore its absence, to toil and travail, spend and be spent, till every one that God hath made of our bone and blood be brought under his hand and stand erect in his place among men, bearing the image of God, is the great labour of every one to whom Christ is precious. In the light of this simple illustration, the following narrative may instruct and encourage the reader. A more clear instance of the work of the Spirit as the grand sculptor of the kingdom of Christ, has seldom fallen under the eye of any observer.

My engagements rendered it necessary I should remove from the city to a village seven miles on the south-west side of it, on the banks of the Thames. A suitable home being procured and my work resuming its usual channel, the disposal of my leisure hours on Sabbath became my next consideration. The exploration of the village as to the moral condition of its people was determined on. This resolution being formed, the next Saturday found me attempting its prosecution. The month of July was in all its glory. In the afternoon, just as it was wearing away among the amber-like tints of a summer evening, I stood cogitating at the gate of my own cottage as to the direction I would take. Looking towards the south, a winding and sloping lane was visible, flanked on either side by a few fine houses, separated from the path through it by high, well trimmed privet hedges, and intersected about its middle by one of England's great railway lines. The seclusion of the walk, the trilling of bird-music overhead and in the hedges, and the effect of the waning sunlight on its simple beauties, decided my choice. Ascending its easy slope, keeping southward, after a moment's pause to allow an express train to pass, I crossed the line, and in a few minutes I reached the highway. On turning my face northward I beheld the village reposing in a kind of valley, with the Thames creeping through it. As seen from my point of view, the village in some measure resembled a fossil lizard, thick and bunchy towards the shoulders, the legs, with outspread toes, at right angles to the body, and the tail curved as in the attitude of resistance. While I gazed for a moment, my eye was arrested by a mass of brick and wooden buildings; at the west end of it was a saw-mill, built of pitched deals; the east was closed by the main and secondary buildings of a large distillery, the front of the whole mass dipping into the Thames. "Well," said I, "yonder is a slice of this lizard-like village, easily manageable by a nice Sunday School worked by half a dozen teachers. If not so occupied already, by the help of God it shall be so. Who knows what work the grand Sculptor of the kingdom of grace may have done, or may yet do in that place!" With these thoughts revolving in my mind I turned to the left, and, entering a narrow lane bearing northward, I bore down on the spot described.

Having reached the saw-mill, and looking eastward, I had the river on the left, and for a quarter of a mile on the right a frontage of dilapidated houses, two storeys high, with courts, densely populated, stretching behind and approached by bottle-necked entrances, the court forming the body of the bottle; and if the reader wishes to complete the image, let him conceive a population of human beings of all sorts and sizes clad in raiment various as the colours of the rainbow, reminding one of those bottle menageries collected by schoolboys from the ponds on our commons, consisting of leeches and lizards, frogs and sticklebacks, eels and beetles—all alive in water and mud. The population of one of these courts was not less various, the natures of its people as unique, and the element they lived in not more pure. Between the river and the houses ran a platform or a pathway, elevated above the bed of the river eight or ten feet, and protected by a facing of stone. When the tide receded, there lay between this facing and the river a bank of oozy mud, a hundred feet wide, rotting in the sun. Along the pathway was a crowd of human beings, children at all manner of games, men smoking at their doors, and dirty women, arms a-kimbo, killing time with gossip, and defiling some neighbour's character with their tongues. High over all rose the drunkard's chorus varied by the rattle of the beer-pot, for, at each end stood a public-house, their benches outside filled with men.

How full of life the whole scene! Like one of

those fly-clouds that swing above and along our streams on a summer night. But there was one difference: in the cloud of life before me every creature was a soul—a being, *worlds* could not buy, *death* could not destroy, and God in his own person *alone* could redeem.

At a loss in what direction to go, or to what hand to turn, and carefully eyeing the noisy crowd before me, I observed a man leaning against a post smoking and alone. Walking softly towards him, I wished him good evening. He took no notice, but seemed lost in a kind of waking dream. His face was directed across the river, the descending sun fell full upon it; his eyes, vacant and meaningless, seemed directed to nothing; his countenance appeared made of bronze, and deeply marked with the small-pox. Thick black crisp locks fell over his low forehead; his bust reminded me of a ship's figure-head that had ploughed the ocean for years. He was enveloped in a blue guernsey, dirty ducks, and laced boots. He was a fierce, foul, heartless man. Such, at least, was my first impression. At last he condescended to notice my salutation.

"Friend, have you lived long here?"

"Why, I have never lived anywhere else."

"Have you any Sunday Schools here?"

"Oh! that's your game, is it? Ask me about these things? As well ask the post there; chaps like me have no time for these matters, we have to work, sir;

the Bible, Sunday Schools, souls, and 'kingdom come,' and these things we leave to parsons and mother Perry down the way. That old river there gives us our bread, and night and day we have to wait on him, sir. He's our Bible, Church, and Sunday School—everything."

"Well, but what for the world to come?" Here he turned a countenance upon me, every feature of which sneered—settled enmity to God hung upon it like a shadow. Laying his hand coarsely upon my shoulder, he said, "I've told you all I know; hook it now to mother Perry's; she knows all these things as well as I know my 'bacca-box."

"Who is mother Perry, friend?"

"Why (something like softness stole over his face for a moment) "she's a poor old soul as bowed as a cask-hoop, who has bothered us chaps for twenty years about our souls, and hell, and heaven, and such like, and she may be seen coaxing our little (here he used a synonyme for children found neither in the Bible nor Bailey) like a hen her chickens when the hawk is near. She takes them to her house, and reads the Bible to them, you know."

This was just what I wanted. I had unexpectedly fallen upon one of those fine old works of the Spirit—an aged Christian. The quaint description of her in no degree lessened my desire to see her, so turning to my friend, I said:—

"Does she live far off?"

"About a stone's throw from where we stand, just in that court where that young 'un is standing."

"Well, I'll go and see her, and now, sir, remember I say there's another river besides the Thames you must find a job upon, if you would ever make a profitable living, become truly happy, and see heaven—the river of the City of God."

Having parted with my friend at the post, I bent my steps towards the little girl pointed out to me. I asked her to show me Mrs. Perry's.

"O, that's the old lady that reads the Bible to us of a Sunday."

"Yes," I replied.

She turned up the narrow entrance of the court, and pointing to a door with a clean step before it, said, "That's it, sir," and disappeared.

Before knocking, I surveyed the court; it was flanked on each side by very old houses, whose windows were broken and stuffed with odds and ends of old wearing apparel, dust bins and stagnant pools made up the other decorations of the place. Some children at play, one or two women at work, were the only tokens of life.

After lifting the knocker, a clean old woman, bowed with years, opened the door, and asked me to step in. The quietness, order, and cleanliness of the house, so different from everything without, was quite refreshing—like a clear fountain of cold water to a weary traveller in a desert at noon. She pointed me to a seat, and quietly settled herself in the old arm-chair. We now faced each other; on the window sill between us was a stocking she had been mending, and the dear old Bible, well-thumbed in every direction, lay open, and her spectacles upon it. I felt I was indeed in the middle of a "Cotter's Saturday Night." She was on the borders of eighty. When young she had been tall and handsome; in features, strong and decided, indicating much decision of character. Her manner was quiet and rather dry. Her whole exterior betokened long departed physical strength, and her countenance much remaining mental vigour. There was a restlessness in the eye when she was struck with any remark, giving it a sparkling appearance, by the light of which you could almost see into her mind and heart, and the depth to which your words had penetrated, and her terse remarks which followed this phenomenon, made one feel as if looking into a kaleidoscope of quaint devices and endless variety. In a word, I had fallen in with quite a character. In some respects she was a remarkable woman. About her whole demeanour, there was massiveness, with dignity. Her piety festooned it with simple graces, reminding you of an old solid garden wall, hung with pendant flowers. Strong, very; yet warm and grand. A cord ran diagonally through the room, on which were hung some bags, making a partition after the style of the tabernacle. On one side of it was a bed, on the other three or four forms.

"Well, mother, can you guess what has brought me to see you?" said I.

"I have not the most distant idea, sir."

"I feel anxious to know the condition of this neighbourhood as to Sunday Schools. How many have you in the district?"

"We have none, sir, except you call my handful of children that occupy every Sunday that corner where you are sitting, a school."

This remark at once explained the diagonal partition of the room, and the use of the cord and the sacks.

"You astonish me!" I replied. "None! no attempts to educate these neglected children?"

"Attempts, did you say, sir?—of these there have been many, and yet one school hath not arisen out of all the bustle. These were like wintry blasts, sharp and short. Like them, too, they died away in the darkness, and all became quiet as before." Here the twinkle of the old saint's eyes added pungency to her remark.

"How long have you been in this neighbourhood?"

"In this house I have been thirty years."

"Has your Sunday School existed long?"

"It's nearly as old as my stay here."

"Indeed, mother: what induced you to commence it?"

"Why, sir, it's with the lives of many of God's children as it is with that of nations: some of their greatest events spring from trifles. I have spent nearly all my days in and about this neighbourhood; my husband, you know, has been the greater part of his life connected with the water, so we have been nearly all our time on the banks of the river.

"Well, one cold winter day, a little girl came to my door, seeking bread, which I gave her, asking her, at the same time, to come in and warm herself. In those days beggars had neither so much brass, nor of the devil, as they have in them now—we could trust them in-doors then. In the course of conversation I learned there were three or four more little ones at home, and that her mother was ill a-bed. I dismissed her, promising to call at her mother's to-morrow. I called, according to promise. It was one of the houses there fronting the water. I found the girl's tale true as far as it went. But, sir, it did not go far enough, for I discovered that her mother was a hard-working proper woman, with four children and a bad husband; striving to do his part and her own—to get bread for their mouths and clothes for their backs—she was worn out and laid on a sick bed. Sad sight; his wickedness and her weakness were making beggars of the children. On leaving her I promised to call the next day. I was much cast down; the state of their souls before God, their temporal sufferings as a family, and the hint the whole scene gave me of a change for the worse in the character of the people of the district, weighed me down with sorrow. Ah, sir, that visit was putting the bodkin to the bone, and told me a sore was there—that the whole ham was in danger. Being young married, my own family—two daughters—were grown up and in place. My husband, from the nature of his employment, was often from home, so I frequently had spare time. When I returned from my visit I sat musing over the fire. A desire to honour my dear Master in the affairs of that afflicted family filled my whole heart. But what to do I knew not. My influence with the rich was nothing. My station was very humble—a waterman's wife. My means were slender. While so engaged, that saying of God's, 'The gold and the silver are mine,' came with great force into my mind. I started to my feet, saying, "Well, if I am poor, and all my kindred poor, my God is rich—yea, the riches of Jesus are unsearchable." I threw myself before him in earnest prayer. There I laid out the whole case before him. Like Hezekiah, I spread the whole letter before his face. Now I waited his blessed will. I felt soothed somehow, and went quietly on with my household duties. As the evening wore on I sat down to read my evening portion from the Word, and, according to custom, I was comparing passage with passage—that, you know, sir, is my only commentary; I have used no other for twenty years. Well, while so employed, my eye fell on our Lord's command to Peter, 'Feed my lambs.' That was a message to me—a burst of sunshine through a rent in the clouds. I resolved on the spot to bring that poor family to my house in the afternoons, and teach them to read and write, and sew, at least."

Here a gleam of that long past day lit up all her face, revealing a big heart full of grace, truth, and tenderness, affecting my mind like one of those soft scenes in a fine transparency.

"From that day they came to me as pupils. They remained till they were able to work and able to read, write, and sew. My success in this family constrained me to visit others, and deal with them on the same plan; and, sir, I have had twenty, aye, thirty little ones, week-days and Sundays, in this very room."

"What fees did you take?"

"Well, sir, my fees were two-fold. First, the consciousness of relieving for an hour or two daily, poor weakly parents of the noise of their little ones; and second, the possibility of turning their young hearts to Jesus, and, so, as far as in me lay, giving them a chance of succeeding in the two worlds, you know—that which now is, and that which is to come. The amount of these fees collected in this little place for thirty years I know not: the great day will make it all clear."

"You must often think about them all, and often ask the question, 'Where are they?'"

"I sometimes have tidings of a few of them now and then. They turn up everywhere; they are scattered over the living world. My scholars are divided between heaven and earth. Some have gone to glory on the wings of the blessed Gospel. Ah, sir, you spoke of fees. I am well paid. Every one at the Great Teacher's feet is a perfect treasure to my poor heart. Often when I look up among the clouds of an evening, as the sun is going down, I imagine I see their curly locks and dimpled faces looking down on me, and I seem to hear them say, 'Come up, mother—do come, there's no sickness, hunger, nor frost here. Jesus, blessed Jesus, is all in all in this home, and we are happy without end.' My poor heart responds, 'A few more sunsets, and I'll lay down my stick, and these old bones will be laid to rest, and I will come up to my Lord and join my band of darlings in their hymns and their happiness.' These, sir, are but my frail heart's dreamings; they are like oil to my weary joints, and when I step out on my visits I clutch my stick all the firmer for them, and I know they make my otherwise crisp words fall soft as snow-flakes among the sorrows of my suffering neighbours. Now, sir, you have got the history of my coming to live here, and how it was I tried to teach."

CHAPTER II.

"YOU seem to have a mixed population here, mother."

"Yes, sir. According to its size we have. In my humble way I think our population is pretty much like that of the cave of Adullam, only there is not a David among us. Our people are either in trouble, discontented, or steeped up to the chin in poverty. They are watermen, costermongers, or vagrants by profession. The houses are next to nothing in rent, and often change hands."

With a smile I replied, "Your locality, from what you have said, reminds me of one of those spots described by naturalists as being frequented during high winds and stormy weather by almost every kind of bird of passage during the season of migration; in these assemblies every sort and size, every hue of plumage and variety of disposition are represented. Let the weather change, they take wing, and are seen in company no more for years—perhaps never."

"You have just hit it, sir. We have some queer birds among us here at times, and on inquiry I find they are generally seeking refuge from a storm. Oh, sir, if we were active for our Lord we should be much on foot, our quiver full of arrows, and hourly drawing the bow at a venture among them before they disperse; no matter who is struck if the bolt stick; the master can follow and secure the game. I am sure the last arrival among us proves your words. One of these little tumble-down houses in the next court was to let. I was visiting a sick neighbour, and on leaving I was standing talking to a member of the family at the door, the person to whom the empty house belongs came up the court, followed by a tall dark man and a delicate-looking boy, both exceedingly well dressed.

Their language and their manner leads me to believe they are gentle folks passing through an hour of trial; if not, they are in some way mixed up with that class. The man is like a foreigner, his accent was strange, in his manner there was haste, and in his eye there was fire. Whenever he spoke to his boy the latter looked up in his face as the oft-beaten dog does into that of a master who can use the whip. While parting with my neighbour they returned from viewing the house. The landlady, as she passed me said, 'Well, I've let my old house at last.' 'I trust you'll have pleasure in your tenant,' I replied. Now, sir, these strangers have been here more than six months; what they are, whence they came, or how they live, no one is able to reveal to this hour. At stated intervals that man and boy are visited towards evening by a tall handsome woman; during her stay with them, which never exceeds an hour, words run high. The boy is often heard weeping, the man conversing in tones so full of anger as to resemble the barking of a dog in a fight, she returning all his taunts upon himself in scorching words amid bursts of hysteric laughter; they then separate, and she glides through the court with the dignity of a duchess. The low mourning words of the boy, and the growling of the man are all that are heard; they too die away, and all is again still. I called one day, but was kept at the door; every word in behalf of the master was rejected; this only I learned, that he was a Romanist. From that day to this these storms arise and die away, but their position is still wrapt in mystery."

"I was right then, mother, as to the place and the character of its people. Oh, would it not be a grand thing if God in his providence were to enable us so to labour as to attract around the cross of our glorious Saviour some of these birds of wandering foot and weary wing?"

"All *I* can do now, sir, is to wish you God speed, and remember you all at a throne of grace. The next school I shall have a part in will be that of my darlings around the throne in heaven. But, sir, begin the work in faith, there will be no lack of attraction; lift up a crucified Lord, He will draw all men unto Him; that's the promise—and you know there is a place for birds of every feather at the foot of the cross. But, sir, remember any other attraction than Jesus on the cross—Jesus carried from house to house, in your teacher's lives will be vain; of every plan let him be the back-bone; thus you'll stand your ground, yea, prevail, and when I'm cold in the clods and my spirit at rest, I may yet take part in a hymn of welcome to some of the broken-hearted poor of these filthy courts. Short of this you may as well try to move the posts of the path with your breath as to touch their heartstrings with anything less than the Christ of the Gospel."

After kneeling down behind the bags, in prayer, commending our scheme, the people, and each other, to Jesus, we parted, resolving to meet often again.

After leaving the old saint's cottage, I returned by the way I came. My whole soul burned with desire to break ground in that little wilderness for the Lord. On the following Sabbath, I gave a narrative of my adventure to the teachers of my Sunday School. Some thought I was foolish; others said many had tried and failed; and all demurred on the score of the character of the place and its people. After all had spoken freely I left this proposition with them, and a week to consider it:—If means of accommodation be provided, and provision made for probable expenses, will any of you help me? My next step was to secure a room, whence we might sally forth upon the ungodliness and ignorance of the district, as from some lonely outpost of an invading army. Many traits of the real soldier meet in the character of a real Christian. In many of the exploits of the Ragged School Mission there is much of the glee and ardour, tactics and daring of a campaign; but we roll no garments in blood, and our weapons are not carnal. Oh, that all knew the joy, the thrilling anxiety, and the glory that crown the struggles of this forlorn hope of the cross! Having a good deal of the old soldier in my nature, I could not keep the military spirit from rising in my breast and bubbling up through all my feelings as I reconnoitered the line of old houses along the river front, with an eye to business, and meditating an attack on the enemy's works, if camping ground could be obtained.

"THAT'S THE TEACHER FOR THEM"

SEE PAGE 37.

I had not gone many steps before I heard the sonorous voice of my friend, in dirty ducks and laced boots. Andrew was his name, I learned. He was in the act of mooring a barge; his work was hard, and his countenance shone in sweat as if anointed with oil. I did not think for a moment he would condescend to notice me again. I was mistaken. He looked irritated and fatigued, and supposed me fair game for a few random shots.

"Well, sir, how goes the school dodge; has mother Perry engaged you to be dry nurse to all the little ——(using his favorite synonyme for children) on the waterside?"

"Yes, Andrew, and I'm on the look-out for a nursery."

"If it be anywhere near me, I'll take my pennyworth of sleep the night before, I know. Such a kettle of fish! My eye! all these brats gathered into one of the mouse-traps up the court. Why, sir, they'll bundle the lot of you out at the window. It won't do, sir, believe me."

"But, Andrew, suppose we try. That is the least we can do, at any rate."

"It has been tried, all have showed the white feather and bolted. Ha, ha, well I never! The idea of teaching and breaking in that 'warmin' along the path there, with prayers, singing of hymns, and the long faces of a few men and women. Look here, sir, (holding up a rope's end) that's the teacher for them, he made me quiet, I know, and clever, too. For them he'll do the same."

"Now, Andrew, that's your plan; here is mine. I want to rent a room; to meet the grown-up people in it once a week for prayer, and on the other evenings of the week to gather the children there, and teach them to read and write, and on the Sunday evenings instruct them in the Word of God."

"That's a nice bill-of-fare. You're kind, sir; but oh, you're soft! aye, as soft as the goods you deal in. Teaching, preaching, and praying for them! The very last things *I* would try; you mean well, but you're green, I can see. Now listen to me. There's the 'Ship' at this end, and the 'Fox' at that (two taverns); first scuttle the one, and then snare the other. That'll be two to one for your prayer meeting; then as for the young 'uns let them hang as they grow awhile, only keep this going among them (holding up the rope), that's the best gospel for them, and if once they taste it, they'll believe it. As for your school, try it after they have been awhile in the one I propose. Now, sir, there's a bit of logic for you, without teaching, preaching, or praying. Good night, sir." So saying, he turned on his heel with a whistle, and left me.

I was puzzled, yet pleased. There was something about him I had not seen before; below his rough manner there was heart; among his crude notions lay sundry shrewd guesses at what was right, and through his conversation there sparkled streaks of wisdom and mother wit. I was struck at meeting him again, and pondered his words. I wandered along the path looking for an empty house, and found one—black as Newgate in its exterior, and through its broken casements the winds had entered many a day. On inquiry I found the landlady, a sharp-faced, little woman—her words a little sharper than her features, and one who could drive a hard bargain, singing the while on a high key the praises of her house. She was a good woman withal, and now is up among Mother Perry's darlings with the dimpled faces. I got the whole house for four shillings a-week. My first glance at its interior I shall not soon forget. Imagine yourself looking into a china shop after a bull had danced a polka in it, and you will have some idea of its internal arrangements. I now summoned my teachers to meet me the next day. All were present, and listened to my second report of the land. Fourteen out of my staff of twenty teachers volunteered. We formed ourselves into a working party. For several weeks we worked like "navvies," white-washing, mending floors, paper-hanging, and furnishing—finally handing it over to the care of a widow with five children, who, for free lodgings, agreed to keep it clean and look after our property. The recollection of our last evening's work, when all was done, even now steals over my memory like music. There we sat, round one of the widow's deal tables, black as sweeps, and, with hymns and prayers, took possession in the name of the Lord.

As the day appointed for opening wore on, my volunteers and I were occasionally visited by feelings peculiar to men at the threshold of an enterprise. Hope supplanted fear, and fear supplanted hope; we took the precaution of having no ladies with us. We met for prayer, and then sallied forth. While yet a far way off a tumultuous sound reached us—the distant roar of a "row;" whistling and cat-calls, mingled with snatches of song, fresh from street, slum, and purlieu, varied with a Babel-like language, as confused and as unholy. Here and there a boxing-match added variety to the scene; men and women peeping out at their doors and windows, some laughing, some jeering, and others swearing; in the distance, friend Andrew leaned against his favourite post at his pipe, his face wrinkled with a contemptuous smile as of a philosopher whose wise counsels had been rejected. And as the fun grew fast and furious around our door, he was evidently calculating the power of his favourite gospel—the rope's end, and how, like oil on the troubled waters, he and it would become were their combined influence turned upon the heaving mass of humanity before him. Our appearance on the scene was the signal for a grand explosion. For a moment we were swallowed up and lost; we were assailed with all the interrogatives and pithy sayings of modern slang. At the window over the door stood our poor little widow with her five children; they were like a group of malefactors about to undergo some sore punishment.

At last, by sheer power of muscle, we got next the door. I was admitted, surveyed our arrangements, and found them complete. We admitted our candidates for religious instruction in pairs till the room could hold no more. To close the door was as hard as to open it. This being achieved, we were now between two fires, one within and the other without. On ascending the stair the scene was lively in the extreme; there, in one ball of life, they rolled about among the benches somewhat like a cluster of mites in a Stilton cheese, as seen through a first-class microscope; whistle, whoop, and yell rose aloft over the whole scene; each teacher as red in the face as a turkey, and our poor widow in a corner with folded hands, one of the most striking portraits of despair I had witnessed for years, only giving signs of life as the crack and smash of her expiring chairs and tables reached her ear.

At last we called upon one of the most experienced of our number to commence; he was a carpenter, with "sinews like iron bands," a clear head, and much tact. He tried, but in vain; his attempts were repelled as rocks fling back the waves. Pausing for a moment, his eye gathering fire, and his cheek gathering blood, he pounced upon one of the ringleaders, and raising him in his powerful grasp, as if to dash him on the floor, he turned all eyes upon himself: silence reigned. Now was the moment. He made the seizing of the boy the introduction and the picture of a stirring anecdote of the lion which, with great skill, he turned into a parable, illustrating the contention of The "Lion of Judah" with the "roaring lion" over a human soul. The attention was complete, and more than one heart was pierced that night. The victory was won—the victory of order. During the whole lesson our only interruptions were from without—the rattling of sand on the window, the rude song, and stray imprecation. Even these at last died away, the intervals between the assaults becoming longer, the only sounds audible being an occasional cry of pain and a galloping of feet. A glance at the window explained all. Here was Andrew in the capacity of self-elected sentinel, hands in pockets, his favourite—the rope—under his arm, and a band of little ragged rogues at a very polite distance beyond. Not a word he spoke, not a step they advanced. Silence was the result of their relative positions. I was much struck with that singular man's mode of showing his regard to what in his conscience he approved, and in his life condemned. The hour of dismissal arrived. How magical in their power and soft in their cadence were the lines of the dear old hymn—

"All hail the power of Jesus' name!"

each strain coming from the lips of forty ragged children, clear, "as wood notes wild." They dispersed in comparative quiet, each with a tract in his hand. All gone, we crept into a corner and renewed our grateful songs and thanks for what had passed. On reaching the door, all had disappeared—Andrew and his rope too. The first attack had terminated in our favour.

CHAPTER III.

HAVING converted our little out-post into a regular citadel, we began to strengthen it by other out-works. A few ladies joined us. A visiting staff was formed. Hence arose Mothers' Meetings and Evening Classes for Girls, with a Sunday School. The place was over-run with our agency. God blessed us in our deed. One class of the population alone stood aloof from every religious effort—the men and women. After a consultation as to the bèst modes of reaching them, it was agreed to try open-air preaching. Preachers, persons to pray and some to sing, were considered essential for a start. After much prayer the hour and power appeared. The whole area of our labours was visited, hand-bills distributed, the open-air sermon was announced. After the Sunday School closed, we adjourned to a deserted spot, a corner formed by the gable walls of two old houses; in front ran a path at right angles to the two approaches to the river; a fence on each side cut off the garden patches and back courts of two lines of houses, one facing the river and the other the main road through the body of the village. This was our church; a chair beside a post was our pulpit; the back windows, garden walks and fences our stalls, aisles, and pews; and the dear old bottle-necked courts our porches. The preacher was in the pulpit, surrounded by a choir composed of the half-tamed roughs of our little school, each with a fly-leaf of hymns in his hand. But where was our congregation? East and west I looked, and north and south, but from no point of the compass came one of Mother Perry's birds of wandering foot and weary wing. The twig was limed, the cage with open door stood near, and the watchers were hard by. The signal was given, up rose a lively song of praise to heaven, led by a dear old saint—a coffin-maker by trade; for years he had made the Bible the forerunner of shovel and shroud, and when laying many a mother's treasure in the cold earth, often in my hearing has the mourning mother said, "Dear old man, you've emptied my arms but filled my heart, for through you, ere my boy went to his long home, he had the hope of a glorious resurrection." There stood our grave musician, warbling hymns like a throstle, tall and thin as a May-pole, with his white cravat and jet studs, through his mild eyes his devout heart looking up to the land where there is no more death, followed in sturdy strains by our scholars. A few of the teachers were distributed as criers along the path and among the courts, to invite the passer-by to try our wares at the little Gospel bazaar now opened in the corner up the way. The rest of the teachers were grouped round the preacher in prayer—dear fellows, their reverend faces and bowed heads preached silent sermons. I could do nothing but join them in prayer to Him in whose hands are all hearts. While so doing the creaking of an opening window pleasingly interrupted us. The same pleasing sound ran along the lines of houses. It was music to our ears; yes, music there is in a creaking window-sash under such circumstances, and at such a moment. In that unwashed dame there, lolloping on the sill beside her unshaved husband, is more of interest than ever looked down from the canvass of Kneller or Reynolds. By-and-bye the garden fences were lined with listeners, and passers-by were stopped at the preacher's chair as chips are by the grating of a mill-pond. We had the right man in the right place that night. On that old oak chair stood a brave, tender-hearted, yet iron-nerved man of God. Thick-set in every limb, one, who amid the light of other days had laid low many a manly form in the dust of the boxing-ring, he was well acquainted with human nature, of vast experience and full of tact; every thought in his robust mind oozing to the surface through a stratum of spirituality. There he stood, love to God and love to man stirring in him "like wind through a tree;" his fine countenance (here and there marked with wounds gotten in other fields than those of the Gospel) reflecting the light of the setting sun, and that of a Sun that knows no setting. Not far from him stood old Mrs. Perry, worshipping, leaning on her staff. Our congregation was now two hundred strong; all deeply attentive. At the foot of the path noise was heard. I trembled for the result. The sermon, I felt, was safe in such hands. I knew my man. But the peace of that crowd of listening souls, the success of our first effort, quivered in the balance. Our preacher, with consummate tact, as if taking a rest, called upon James, the sweet singer of our Israel, to raise a hymn. The glorious strains of "I lay my sins on Jesus," burst from all around with much power, and rising aloft above the distant din, preserved peace for the moment. I, under cover of the music, wore down the road in the direction of the noise. If I could not quell it, I thought I might play the decoy duck, and wear it away, at least, into a place better prepared for it. I had not gone far before I came upon a group of men opposite the "Ship" public-house. Intense anger burned in all their faces, and the language of violence was on their lips—each man's clothes as if flung on him with a pitch-fork. Two of the group leant over the water-trough—their backs were towards me. The laced boots and ducks told me Andrew was one of them. He was in the act of washing the other's face. Andrew, as he laved the water in his neighbour's face, was saying, "I told you not to do it; he that insults me must remember I'm my own hammerman, and can make dints on the dial of any man in England, aye, and my bit of smith's work is so well done, too, that they don't return to my forge for many a long day, nor will you, I know. There now, old boy, you're as clean as a ribbon, and your cheeks as plump as prize pork. On with your toggery, give us a grip of your hand, and if you're satisfied so am I. Will you have a drop of anything? if so, come on, then go home to the old girl and help to nurse the kids." When Andrew looked up his face was smeared with blood and swollen; the delirium of conquest playing in every feature. They all disappeared into the tavern, and the crowd dispersed. After a little time, as I was leisurely returning to our preaching station, some one behind me called out my name. I looked round; Andrew was at my side; blood on his face and hands; with the utmost coolness he said—

"Well, sir, how did you get on at the mouse-trap to night?"

"None the better for *you* or your gospel to-night," I retorted.

He replied, "I was teaching a little myself to-night, sir."

"If so, Andrew, it was not the gospel of peace."

"Well, sir, I don't know *that;* my pupil will not disturb *my* peace for a long while, and the lesson I have just given him will make him very peaceable everywhere for some time, so you see my gospel can make peace, too, and yours can do no more."

"Ah, but Andrew, the peace our gospel makes is everlasting; breaks no bones, blackens no eyes, and makes its possessor a peace-maker wherever he goes."

"Well, sir, I have been a peace-maker these many years; I have made peace with every cove on the water-side, and without preaching, praying, or the magistrate. I have a plan of my own, I have always told you so. It is this, sir; if a man is troublesome to me, I warn him—that's lesson first; if he refuse, can't take it up, having always with me a couple of stunning teachers, who never fail in making the thing clear, *they* give the second lesson. My pupil then picks up for himself all the following lessons as easily as putting peas in your mouth. I'll introduce you to my teachers if you like. (Here he held up both his hands, filthy with the gore of his last fray.) These are the gentlemen, aint they like their work? So on the score of peace-making I am on equal terms with you."

"But, Andrew, your peace-making leaves no love behind; it stings like a serpent and bites like an adder."

"That may be; but this I know, sir; not one of all these you saw at my last peace meeting will either sting or bite me."

"True, Andrew, but they have the will if not the power."

"Well, sir, grant it; pluck out their stings and draw their teeth; you'll cure them."

"But, Andrew, you never touch the heart by your plan, it's always left the same—hateful and hating."

"Yes, sir, but I never go so deep as that. What have I got to do with a man's heart? Ain't a man's heart like his house? I've no right to go there unless invited; and besides, I do not know under what button of his waistcoat that thing lies which you call a heart, and which teachers and parsons make such a mighty fuss about; it's quite enough for me, sir, that I look after the stings and teeth; if they keep their own place, the heart may go to Putney for me."

"Andrew, the peace Jesus brings goes direct to the heart. Gentleness, love, and mercy towards all men, flow forth of him who has it. The man that is enjoying it is never happy except he is doing some one a good turn. Ay, Andrew, if he could he would carry all men from this world of woe up to heaven, the palace of the God of peace. For that purpose he desires to live; it is his meat and drink so to do. Will you become a member of *our Peace Society?* Jesus waits—ay, waits for you. O man, look up and see the wounds he has gotten in making our peace. He has done all the fighting, Andrew. You need study war no more. Leave the ring and join us, there's an opening for you."

Here, pulling himself up, knitting his lips as if for one great effort, he turned round and laid his hand on my shoulder, and replied, "Ay, ay, just as I said at first; soft, very; yes, green as one of Mother Perry's cabbages. Sir, I always like to help them that can't help themselves; for instance, I carry the water and fuel of the old wives on the walk there when I have a chance, and now I'll take your little can out of your hand, and your small bag of fuel on to my shoulder once more; but if you won't do what I bid you, I'll leave you as the boys do a puppy they're drowning, to lie where the string and the stone will lay you. Now listen, sir. When your teaching and preaching are all over, what will *you get?* Lots of bad breaths up in the mouse-trap. Lots of "chaff," mixed with brick-bats and mud, in the open air. Lots of yarns on the same key as the song of a puppy when its mother's out. Soon as you're gone the chaps will pitch on one side their long faces, as a London Bridge beggar does his legs and arms when he joins his pals at night. I know 'em. You ain't the cove for us; you want brass, you want 'nouse.' Let me amongst the youngsters with my rope, and I'll make them fit for the world. Let me on the chair up there, and one of my sermons will serve them for a month. I know the text that will suit them. Just give me the beer bill of the "Ship," or a leaf from the night-book of the station-house. My eye! how impressed they would be; how quietly they would disperse; no yarns, not one puppy song that night, I know."

Here a curious phenomenon appeared. The day had been hot and sultry; towards evening a few thunder clouds began to sail through the sky; while speaking to me, a peal of thunder rolled gently over head. Andrew looked at me. "Now, sir, did you hear that?" he said; "well, that's the preacher I always listen to. I don't like him; you never know where *his* remarks are to fall, or what is to follow." He was trembling all over. While shaking my hand, he said, "Good night, you gospel chaps have the better of me in thundery weather." He darted off like a bird, through the garden, up the court, and was lost in the house. On inquiry, I found he had from his boyhood manifested similar aversion to thunder. I had often read of the aversion of some men to one or other of the great elements of nature; an instance so striking I had never seen. I lost the close of his lecture, but his last words struck me much; they were the testimony of an uneasy conscience to that inestimable peace the Spirit brings, and its preciousness in the hour of mortal terror.

By this time the night was far spent, and on reaching the preaching station they were singing a parting hymn. Dear old James wore a smile on his face now; the work was done; the people gave token in their looks, something had been said which made them think; and our preacher leant against the post, his eyes closed, his anxious soul discoursing with the principalities and powers of another and a better world. The last notes having died away, the people were dispersing quietly, and our teachers mingling among them in friendly talk, when my eye caught in an obscure corner the mysterious man and his boy. By a little tact I reached them and drew them into conversation, which ended in an invitation to visit them in the course of the week. This was my first personal interview with the hero of my narrative. The preachers now adjourned to their little school, and after thanks, praise, and prayer, they separated; full of faith in the future.

After the toil of the week had closed and I was released from duty, I set out, on the afternoon of the next Saturday, to fulfil my engagement with my mysterious friend and his boy. The day was calm, clear, and hot. Having reached the door of his dwelling, I took a hurried glance at its exterior. A few yards round were swept and clean, the door-knocker bright, burnished, and shining in the sun; the window was hung with crimson curtains edged with yellow, and a muslin blind topped with a slip of brass covered the lower part of the sash; compared with the broken glass and coat-stuffed windows of the dwellings around, theirs looked quite aristocratic. The reserve of its occupants, the twilight visits of the duchess-like dame, and the storms of wrath that filled the house during her stay; these all floated in my memory, and filled my mind with feelings akin to those of the man who, amid the sombre atmosphere that precedes a thunder-storm, presents himself at a cottage door in some lone place for shelter. With such feelings I lifted the knocker of that man's door. This was followed by a noise from within as if from the pushing of chairs, pulling of boxes, and the jingling of crockery; a few minutes elapsed, and I was admitted. I mounted the stairs and reached the apartment with blood-coloured curtains. Behind them sat two miserable beings half naked, and with no furniture save three chairs, a huge box, a pallet of straw covered with some old coats, and a few broken cups and saucers; the floor marked here and there with lines, as if some heavy things had been drawn across it. I was asked to sit down. I did so, and on either side of me sat these two wizard-like souls. The face of the man was like an old weather-beaten obelisk, furrowed here and there with many a storm; his eyes dark and glittering, like the surface water of a deep draw-well, at the bottom of which lay many a noisome thing; his hair, long, lank, and black, hung over his Italian features; his teeth white as milk, and his chin covered with a dark crisp beard. His restless eye, his ever moving limbs, reminded one of some denizen of the forest, on the chain and behind the bars. His home, his person, all about him called up in the spectator feelings somewhat like those which rise when in some country parish his ear is startled with the knell of some funeral bell. There is a death somewhere, rises to his lips, and he feels solemnized; so said I, so did I feel. There is a death somewhere. Where? Down at the bottom of that man's heart is death, and its slime is on its strings. Something within me said so. On my right sat the youth, clean in his person, his long jet hair flung back and displaying an ample forehead surmounting finely marked features; his eyes large and dark, soft and floating in a chastened light; his countenance imploring and pensive, indicative of a mind of considerable power, but cowed and crushed by some influence not at first apparent. He was still as a statue. He seemed one of those beautiful and delicate clinging flowers which some rude blast had blown from the wall and rolled in the mud, its graspers yet green, but every prop and stay far away. O how my soul yearned to play the gardener to that tender plant, gather up its crushed tendrils and fix them around Jesus, the only prop for the bruised heart. Ah, my dear boy, the Man that is a hiding-place from the storm and a covert from the tempest is the friend for you.

"Well, my friends," I said, "I feel pleased you have allowed me to call upon you."

The man replied, "I have not heard such an expression in this house since I came to it. They that visit me speak other words and use other names for me than friend. Their pleasure is in my sorrow; they have taken the things out of my house, and with them my character. Nothing is left me but my life. I am alone in the world. This life is but a dreary wild, every man and woman on it a wolf to me."

Here he looked as one who finds his best friend in a glittering blade—a place of lasting repose under the middle arch of some bridge. His attitude was everything a hater of his species could wish for—the fiery eye, the sneering lip, the grinding teeth, and the clenched fist. At that moment the soul of this forlorn man could have danced on the tombstone of a world, and that world, as it appeared from the window of the ark, would have been to his eyes a thing of beauty, and to his heart a joy for ever. The poor boy looked up, trembled, and crept near me.

"But, friend," I said, "you look at all men from one point of view. You measure their feet by the shoes of the few you may have injured, or who in their turn may have done you wrong. To live at all in peace, we must learn to forget and forgive; as our heavenly Father is willing, for Christ's sake, to forgive us."

He said, "What is the use of speaking to me of Christ? It's no good. Some men, *even*, despise me because of a few things they know in my life; and what hope have I from Him who knows all? They who ought to befriend me, because of the past, do not know me in my present misery; and one there is who should have stood shoulder to shoulder with me in this hour of trial, who visits me only now and then, and that to insult me—yes, sir, to sprinkle salt upon my sores. No, sir; for me mercy there is none, not a drop in the breast of a mortal I know. As for Christ and religion, prayer and the Bible, heaven and rest—from all I have sought relief, and found none. No, sir; I can see it, but it is not near. My soul craves for it, but between relief and me there are the ribs of an iron cage—we never meet. There is a gulf between it and me, but no plank spans it, across which my weary soul could crawl. I have given all up. No one cares for me now, and I care for no one. Like a wrecked ship, I'm drifting all alone—to destruction. I've lost my day. The tide in my affairs is settling in broken water. I'm a ruined man."

I felt quite dreary in my own spirit. All I had said disappeared like the snow-drop in the river. Rising to take my leave, I said, "I will not salt your sores, I would like to pour oil into them. Here is a drop of the beaten oil of the Sanctuary. Let it sink to the bone. "Come now, and let us reason together, saith the Lord: though your sins be as scarlet they shall be as white as snow: though they be red like crimson, they shall be as wool." That's a message from God to thee. Will you grant me one favour? Will you come to our open-air sermons, and will you allow your boy to join our Sunday School?" He hesitated, then said, "Leave the matter with myself." I said I would, and left him.

CHAPTER IV.

FREQUENTLY, after our first interview, we met while the open-air services lasted and often got into conversation; but reserve, cold and compact, was interposed between us as a shield; no gladiator in the arena of old Rome could parry a blow with more skill than he could any question he wished to remain unanswered. The boy was allowed to visit occasionally our little school—nearer acquaintance was somehow impossible. To us, as teachers, father and son were emphatically children of the mist.

Because of my other engagements, after a few years' labour, I was removed to another locality. But I had the pleasure of seeing our little outpost on the Thames before leaving it filled by some sturdy friends of the cause, and all its concerns presided over by a young godly minister and his wife. And now, after several years, it still holds out its "beacon ray" among the same people, and the souls of those bottle-necked courts and that oozy walk between the 'Ship' and the 'Fox' are daily fed and prayed for. Best of all, some of them are now in heaven that met me on my first exploratory visit with a lifetime's sins, unforgiven, upon their souls. From time to time I hear of its people and their labours, and often do I remember Mother Perry's birds of the wandering foot and the weary wing.

One morning just after family worship I was called to the door. How I stared to behold Zuccani! the son of our mysterious friend. He was a tall young man now; his eyes still floating in their chastened light—but sunk and hollow; his cheeks emaciated and flushed; his forehead, lips, and chin, of a cream colour; and his nose as if it had been pinched by powerful fingers. Over his whole countenance was spread that imploring look as when first I saw it, and his manner forcibly reminded me of the clinging plant rolled in the mud—it was there still, but prop and stay far away. I shook his clammy hand and invited him in. As I took one look more, I saw consumption was about to mark him for her own if he was not immediately cared for, and I felt unutterably sad. I asked all to retire from the room. His elbow rested on a small table before the library window; and supporting his head on his hand, he looked me in the face and burst into tears. He tried to speak, but emotion made it impossible. At last he muttered, "Here again, sir."

"Can I do anything for you, Zuccani?" I asked.

"Yes, sir, you can save my life and prolong that of my dying father."

Shortly after I had left the locality the father had become a victim of consumption, and now by slow degrees his life was wearing to its close.

"How?" I exclaimed, my mind running to all the ends of the earth—"how, my boy?"

"Sir, will you write a letter for me—at least copy one which I have scratched down; for, sir, I can neither write nor read," (here he pulled out two or three sheets of crumpled post, stitched together with black thread). I tried to read what he had written, but in vain; the inscriptions on the walls of an Egyptian tomb were as clear to me as were the utterances of that bruised soul as they lay in cipher on the sheets of that queer letter.

Thus much I learned from it, at least from his translation of it, that before me stood a youth with a story in his breast which, if unfolded, would glorify God, reflect honour on the Ragged School Movement, and reveal one of those peculiar modes by which the Spirit at sundry times leads sinners to the Cross, for I could distinctly see God was dealing with him.

"To whom do you wish this letter to be sent, Zuccani?" I asked. Here he named one of those remarkable men whom we occasionally meet with among the commercial aristocracy of the metropolis; a man of the deepest piety, the highest intellect, and most commanding position as to influence and wealth—one of those masses of salt that keep sweet and fresh the sweltering bulk of the body mercantile. In a word, he wished our common friend to know the story of his life, and to employ his influence to give him, as he touchingly said—"to give him one chance to stand up in life on his own feet, if he got better."

"Well, Zuccani," I replied, "as far as I have power with our friend I will use it for you, but I think you would better leave it till to-morrow, and I will take the particulars from your own lips." I wished him to compose his weary heart and rest his wasted frame for a day; for during the conversation his countenance had assumed the appearance of one that is hovering on the brink of eternity, and go when he would, must take your heart with him; and there was a "dead set" in his shining eye, which, when hid from yours, made you feel as if you were suddenly left in the dark. He was persuaded, and spent the day with us; we parted in the evening, he promising to return to-morrow.

According to promise, he called at ten the following morning. We retired to a back parlour lighted from the roof; having quietly settled down facing each other, I said, "Well, Zuccani, why do you wish to put our friend in possession of your personal history?"

"I have many reasons, sir, which my conduct, I hope, will declare better than my words. It is right, sir, to be honest—to speak with the lip exactly what you feel in your heart. Well, I earnestly desire you to do this kindness for me, simply to enable me, if God will, to come out into life in some honourable way; I am tired living behind backs. Oh, if I were strong again, and had some healthy work to do, I would feel I was somebody! as it is, I have seen so much of misery, and felt so much of it, that I almost beg people's pardon for being in the world at all. I feel as if I had stumbled into it by a mistake, people make me feel I am so much in the way." As the wine sparkles in the crystal goblet, so did the blood mantle in his almost transparent cheek, while he spoke. And from behind his hollow eye looked out on me a man, a *bonâ fide* man, bruised and broken to be sure, but nevertheless a man; and from out that skeleton came such a cry for a little fair play in the battle of life that one was bound to listen, and as "he held you with his glittering eye" a desire to help him seemed all you could be conscious of. I intuitively exclaimed, "Have then your wish, my boy, in God's name!" Stooping forward, he became absorbed in prayer. I disturbed him not. He was evidently collecting himself—bracing himself up. Meekly and quietly he looked up and said, "Now, sir, I am ready to reply to all your questions; but you know I am no scholar. You can put my words together and read their meaning."

Here commenced the first of a series of conversations, which has enabled the author to present the reader with the following narrative.

"Well, Zuccani, who, or what was your father?"

"He was a gentleman's servant. My grandfather was an Italian, and earned his living as a teacher of dancing in London. My mother is an Englishwoman, from the county of Norfolk. My father and she met in service, being both employed by one master."

"What kind of a person is your mother, Zuccani?"

"She is, or at least was, considered a fine woman; but hard work, broken spirits, and many sorrows have altered her appearance. Yet, even now, she is a tall, powerful woman, with a will of her own strong as iron. I used to think, from the few glimpses I got of her in my childhood, mother was fit only to be a lady, and one of the earliest expressions of my lips was, "Father, don't she look nice!" But sir, looks are not love; neither does fine stature make a mother. A kind heart with love in it, a quiet home and will to work for it, and faith in Jesus, that's the stuff REAL fathers and mothers are made of; all others are shams. At least, so I think."

"Zuccani, you seem to have had a hard lot in your younger days; where were you born?"

"My lot has been hard, but, ah! sir, all for the best, I believe. I was born in a narrow street running off one of the main thoroughfares of the north of London."

"How were you brought up?"

"For ten years after my birth my mother stayed at home, and acted as laundress to the family where my father was in service."

"Had you a happy home then?"

"My recollections of it are very dim, but two of them I have carried with me to this hour; yes, sir, and they will go with me to the grave; they used often to cross my mind when at play; they were the first links of that chain of affliction which, ever since I recollect, has bound every member of my unhappy home."

"What might they be, Zuccani?"

"When but a child I used often to puzzle my mind, sir, why it was that our house was no meanly furnished; and, when father came to see mother, what it was that made him all at once spring up, and, with one flourish of his hand, sweep all the little ornaments from the mantelpiece and send cups and saucers spinning out at the window, his eyes glancing like flames. Often did I sit at the root of a tree in the garden asking the question, what these things meant, crying and chewing my pinafore; then I would dart into a crowd of playfellows and try to forget; but often, between me and the sky, I would see, like a dark shadow, my father. I would stand dead still for a moment, amid the fun and fury of the game, rub my eyes and look up, and run off to play again. Another scene is burned into the very centre of my heart, sir—their quarelling. Often did words run high towards evening; from words they would sometimes proceed to a struggle. Often have I been thus aroused from my sleep, and in terror hid my face in the bedclothes, and wept and prayed; or, so frightened was I sometimes, I would spring naked to the floor and creep into a corner, and, falling on my knees, pray aloud. More than once their seeing me so employed has hushed them to silence. That unfurnished room, these whirlwinds of anger, are my earliest recollections of home. Awfully dull did they make the days, the long days, the dreary days I had to sit at the fireside. At last, sir, that fireside was deserted, its fire put out, and home I had none for many a day. I have lived with the stranger for years. That very day you saw us looking at the house in the court was the closing stage of a long journey among strange faces, and with people of cold hearts."

"But why, Zuccani, did father and mother live so unhappily?"

"Sir, it pulls the strings of a son's heart to lift the veil from off the frailties of a father and a mother.

Drink, company, and temper on father's side; a sense of neglect preying on a high spirit, a warm heart, and an iron will on that of mother. These things made my boyhood all bitterness, and cast my lot among strangers. To use an expression of mother's, that "Italian extrac" of my father filled a bitter cup for her, and shaped a rough path for me. But, sir, it's all for the best. Allow me to leave this part of my story. Father and mother have many things in their character for which I love them, and they are my parents."

He sat for a moment staring on vacancy. His whole soul was in the power of memories that tried it to the uttermost. Like a swimmer sitting on the beach after buffeting a strong current, he seemed weary and worn. Glad was I to hear the dinner-call sounding in the hall. We adjourned to dine, resolving to return to the narrative in the afternoon.

According to agreement we met in the back parlour in the afternoon. So indelibly had succeeding events engraven themselves on his memory, so completely and distinctly had almost every person in the succeeding part of the narrative performed their part in his troubled life, that as he proceeded in his account he preserved their very looks, gestures, and words; so that the author had little difficulty in presenting to the reader each individual, acting for him and herself, in their own character. During that afternoon and evening was displayed before me a remarkable instance of the power of affliction to reveal passing events in light so intensely clear, that they seem to burn their way into the very texture of the mind itself, and there remain, painfully exact in every particular. The photography of affliction is done by fire. You have only by a simple act of memory to bring the soul on whose remembrance these pictures are burned, to the hour and day when first they were put there, and immediately you awaken in the eye the wild light, bring to the cheek the blush of boiling blood, and raise the defiant curl to the lip, characteristic of human nature in the day of oppression. You call forth all the faculties in a state of white heat, giving a pathos often melting, to the simple utterance of the affections, as if the hour and power of the trial was again upon the sufferer; who, simply because he cannot help it, speaks forth his sorrow in language of such unnatural brilliance that it works upon you and in you like a charm. Poor Zuccani that afternoon produced before me every spot and scene he had passed through so clearly, as to make me feel as if I had been carried thither; gave each actor his and her place in them so simply, so vividly, that I felt as if I had been personally introduced to them, and thus I have been able to sketch each locality as it now stands in its place in the metropolis, and each individual as though he had been sitting for his portrait to *me*. Oh, the minuteness, the faithfulness, the fiery rigour of affliction!

"Well, sir," commenced Zuccani, "things at home

were now coming to a pass; something had to be done for a living. Both my parents had resolved to make some change in their work and way, so as to earn more money. Meanwhile a little brother was born, who only lived a few months. This birth and death brought a crisis. My parents had never learned any trade. Work as domestic servants in some gentleman's house, or want, were the two alternatives, under present circumstances, which stared them in the face. And mother, like father, had resolved on the former. But they could not obtain employment under the same roof, therefore separation for a season must take place. Amid tears, accusations, and regrets, it was resolved that for a time we should cease to exist as a family. During one of the conversations on the subject, the only one I was permitted to hear, and that simply because it was high time I should do so, as the last day I was to be in a home with them for years had arrived, I waited till they were silent, and, looking up, I said, 'And with which of you am I to go?'

"'You, my boy'—here both turned upon me their faces wet with tears—'You, Zuccani,' said father, 'are to be sent to lodgings; there you are to be trained to one of the finest professions in London.' Both again burst into tears and sobs.

"'If what you are to train me to, be so nice, why does it make you weep?'

"'Hush, Zuccani, you shall know all to-morrow. A lady and gentleman will call here to-morrow, who will take you to their house, where, as I said, you will be trained, taught, and made a gentleman.'

"Now it was my turn to weep. I flung my arms round mother's neck and asked, 'Am I never to see you again?' and wept bitterly.

"'Yes, my darling boy, often will you see me,' she replied, 'but you know we are very poor, and we are going out to work for you, to make money, and then we will take and furnish a house, and you shall come home again; by that time also *you* will be making money yourself, and when we are all at home again we will be so happy.'

"I doubted, and from her manner she herself was anything but sure. My poor young soul was hovering on the edge of that desert through which I have passed, and that speech of mother's told me its Arabs were near; for, sir, there was but one day between me and a life among strangers for three miserable years—among the Arabs of London. Little did I sleep that night; often did I sketch the portraits of the lady and gentleman expected on the morrow, and deeply did I ponder the nature of that profession that was to make ME a gentleman, and as father did not say what it was, my suspense was intense. We were all early up the following day, and the house put in order—nothing but tears and silence reigned. As for me, sir, I moved about as if in an hour I was to be slain. I was slain—my soul was, that day's deed murdered *it* outright. Had it not been for your Ragged School and these open-air sermons, my heart would never have come to life again. I was sad, sat down on a chair, looked to the ceiling, and cried. Mother sat opposite to me, and she was dumb. Father gazed out at the window, and now and then broke the quietness by mutterings, the meaning of which I could not catch. The knocker at last proclaimed the arrival of our visitors. We all started—were on our feet in a moment, just as if life had entered a number of statues in one of those yards on the New North Road, and set its stone women, shepherds, and little praying sailor-boys all a-reeling through each other. The blackest day I have ever seen had come, the coldest hearts I have met in my life were on my father's threshold!"

CHAPTER V.

"In they burst. 'How goes it, Footy (the name he often used for father), to-day; and, madam, how are you? and Zucci, I hope I see you well. No; you all look as if you had Calcraft's ribbon round your necks.' Such were the first words that fell from the lips of our gentleman visitor: a little spare man; his eyes grey and glancing, they seemed to follow you everywhere. He could speak with them, laugh with them till they faded into two dark strips, rule man and beast with them, do everything with them but weep; that he could not do; that he never did. In his whole flesh moisture there was none: it was as yellow and as dry as that of a mummy from Egypt. His lips were thin and pale; his hair hung in long ringlets, dark and oily, all round his head; his brow was furrowed with lines, and across these ran a vein or two, swollen and blue; he had no beard, and was a little below the middle size.

"'Why look so sad, Footy? that little scrap of humanity will be all right with me. You have got a fine field before you once more: no count, no care, but simply to look after the old merchant's idiot son, referring to father's new situation. Walk him well, and he'll sleep; feed him well, and he'll love you; thump him well, and he'll obey you. Why, man, cheer up and look out. Pitch overboard all your soft goods, such as love and fear—the whole nest of affections—make a clean breast of *them*. I have murdered these innocents long ago, and looking to number one, have cried before all men, 'Gain, be my Lord; for I will worship thee!' Be a man, old chap, and go ahead. Aint these the counsels for Footy, mother? Have they not made your little evil seed all he is?' Here he looked up into the old lady's face, waiting for her nod, conscious of having said something that would have graced the lips of Solomon.

"'Yes, child; your own good parts and my training have done it; and your present position proves it has been well done.'

"His mother was a woman between fifty and sixty, short and stout, red and puffy of countenance, with a large forehead surmounted with fine dark hair, here and there dashed with grey; from under protruding eyebrows stared out upon you two eyes, dark as sloes, that seemed to understand everything that came before them by reading it, and when read, to know exactly what it was worth, and when, and where, and how to use it in fighting her way through life. When roused by anger, her eyes seemed to blaze, which, when added to the natural radiance of her face and the bitter sayings of her tongue, made her at such seasons an object to be dreaded. In her sunny moments it was a task to love her. When she laughed, her chin and cheeks dimpled. In conversation her whole person was called to the work, winking with either eye, raising her whole face to heaven. At times the conversation would leave her lips, and take refuge among her fingers and feet. A story told by her somehow stuck to you. She could swear, and did do it; she knew her Bible, and often quoted it; she loved drink, and nicknamed it the 'skyey influence.' Often, sir, at all the hours on the face of the clock, have I had to trudge the lanes of London to procure her this abominable 'influence.'

"Turning to her son, she said, 'While arranging matters, let Zucci bring us in a drop of 'skyey;' it will oil all the wheels, and everything will move without noise to its place.' I was accordingly despatched for the precious 'influence.' When I returned the conversation was changed, but I could see by my parents they had been doing in my absence something which their poverty more than their wills rendered necessary. Yes, sir, I was handed over on that day to be trained for the stage as a dancer by one of those desperate characters that are adored behind the curtains of our second-rate theatres. On that day it was also agreed that for a long and dreary season I was also to have a change of a mother, and my new mother was one of the most remarkable women for cunning, coarseness, and ability, I have ever seen. If living with a person photographs their likeness on the heart, I am sure I have one of the most remarkable female miniatures there ever worn by a man; and there, sir, I fear it will remain all my stay here below, ay, even up to the very judgment. Oh, sir, I can see her now, as Macbeth saw the ghost, in all places and among all kinds of people. Yes, sir, while talking to you I see her in some scenes in her dingy house, and at this hour they sadden my heart. At last the party broke up. He and his mother were the worse for the 'skyey influence,' and, judging by their talk, they were under another influence that did *not* come from the skies. As he passed me he chucked me under the chin, and slipped a shilling into my hand, saying, 'Now, my boy, I'll make a gentleman of you. I'll call for him to-morrow evening in a cab, and drop him at mother's on my way to the theatre. So saying, he left the house; from that moment, sir, was opened the darkest chapter in my life; but it's all for the best.

"Father and mother had been so far successful as each to get a situation in very respectable families. My father was to be the keeper of an idiot lad, the son of a merchant: my mother was to assist in the nursery of a lady of rank. Our respective homes were to be wide apart. Father was to be in the extreme south-west of London, mother far toward the north-west, and I was to be buried in a lane in the south-east. Each was to be separated from the other by miles on the morrow, to rejoice or to sorrow apart. A few hours before the break-up we spent together: silence, sadness, and tenderness was the rule of the house for the time. Had the tenderness of that short period been spread over the bygone years of our family life, separation would never have darkened our door. I received a great many instructions as to my conduct towards my superiors, and both parents painted a very bright future for me. But, sir, our domestic dream was scattered by the loud rattle of the door-knocker. The little actor was there, all in a bustle, not a moment to spare. After a shower of kisses and many tender embraces from my parents, all of a tremble I found myself and my little bundle at the foot of the stairs, and bathed in tears I buried myself in a corner of the cab. After some whispers between my parents and Murray (the actor's name), the cab started, and I was launched into the world. During the ride he tried to comfort me; but finding it useless, he gave it over. Looking up once or twice through my tears, I could see his little grey eye rolling and staring at the roof of the cab, his lips muttering great swelling words, and his hands and feet placed as if he was in a struggle or an agony. This increased my terror, and led me to believe I was in the power of a man run stark mad. He was not mad; this was simply his mode of rehearsal; I was soon accustomed to it. My eye also discovered two old swords, two or three masks, and some black and yellow robes glittering with spangles, in another corner of the cab. The conduct of Murray during the journey, the questionable instruments, the grim countenances of the masks, and the spangled dresses, made such a dreary impression on my mind, which, added to my own sorrow, made me crouch myself up into a corner, and in childlike resignation await the issue. After turning down a long narrow lane, crooked, dark, and dirty, just immediately before a dingy arch, the cab pulled up opposite a low mud-spattered door, which immediately opened, and on its step stood Mrs. Murray, puffy and red, dimpled and terrible, as when I first saw her. As he handed me over to her he said, 'Here he is, a regular sponge, full of crystal waters; a bottle of tears. He and the blue bottle of "skyey" together will make grog to both of us for a week. All right, cabby. One o'clock, mother.' Away he rolled, and the door closed on the old lady and me.

"I looked up in her face, then all around me. I found myself standing in a large room, covered with a crimson carpet, and lighted by a gas pendant from the centre of the ceiling; a brisk fire burned on the hearth, and a huge black cat lay dozing before it on the rug. Masks and fiddles, robes and swords sparkling with spangles, hung on the walls. A little table, covered with blue, stood in the centre of the room. It and a few chairs completed the furniture of the apartment. I sat down on a little chair near the fire, and having dried up my tears, I was silent and somewhat sullen.

"'Well, Zucci, I hope you will like your new home—won't you? I am now to be father and mother to you, all in one;' and, so saying, she drew me to her and asked me to kiss her and prove a loving son, as her own dear little Murray had done for years. I drew back; I could not help it. I would sooner have kissed the old black cat at my foot; her big red face and sharp eyes looked so queer, so stupid, when she tried to be loving—to her such a feeling was not natural.

"'You little dainty-livered milksop, you refuse me a kiss, do you? Indeed; what next! The little fellows up the court sell their soft wares cheaper. See how they hold up their little lips with delight; and sweet are their kisses, too—each mouth just like a split cherry, wet with heaven's own dew.'

"'Ah, but, Mrs. Murray, it's not so new to them as to me; their fathers and mothers kiss them all day long: I have no parents, and strangers never kiss me.'

"'Do you think me a stranger? I have been no stranger to your father and mother, at any rate, you little dainty chops. Come, kiss me this moment, and be friendly.'

"This she said in such a tone, and with such a stare, as made me tremble. I crawled towards her, and presented my cheek, which she kissed, muttering as she did it, 'Ay, refuse affection to her who has kept your parents from the union, and yourself from the streets!' My obedience seemed to melt her. An icicle dropped into the fire could not have melted sooner. The first hour I lived with her she made me feel her will was of iron, and that the word of her mouth was a law. If obedient to her desires, she could be soft—even tender—but if you differed from her, the words of her lips rattled about your ears like bits of flint and steel. I never forgot this first hour's teaching; it was one of those blows in a fight which is half the battle. I carried this first night's lesson with me through all my after-career under her roof.

"After painting in bright colours my future, and compelling me to devour a little supper—more from fear than appetite—I was lighted up-stairs to a little garret containing a chair, a table, a mirror, a wash-hand-stand, and a little iron bedstead with a yard of carpet before it. I was told it was to be my bedroom.

"'Now, strip,' she said, 'and I'll take your candle away.' I stood for a moment, as if hesitating. She gave me one of those stares which all who were in her power well understood. I said, 'You may take the light away; I'll slip to bed in the dark; to that I have been accustomed.'

"'What are you to be up to, eh?' she asked.

"'Nothing,' I simply replied: 'I would like to say my prayers before lying down, that's all, Mrs. Murray.'

"'Oh, that's all, is it—some of your Sunday School manners—ha, ha, ha! Ay, just as Murray said, there must be a soft spot about you, and I suppose it's from that quarter you fill your eyes with tears. That's all past now. In a short time you'll be a man, and must leave all these nursery tricks to those little fellows that are washed and combed at certain hours, and drummed to school on Saturdays and Sundays with cakes and kisses. In a day or two you will have to appear before hundreds, dressed in a spangled robe, to dance and sing for your supper. Come, begin at once to be a man, and tumble into bed without nursery rhymes or playing games at folding hands. These are baby tricks.' She prevailed, and I was laughed out of my prayers. I got into bed, was left in the dark, where, after tossing about awhile, crying and praying at intervals, I fell asleep.

"Such was my first night away from home on my

"SHE PREVAILED — AND I WAS LAUGHED OUT OF MY PRAYERS"

SEE PAGE 7[illegible]

own account. Stifling prayer was my first preparatory lesson for the stage. And let them who long for it remember, a prayerless heart is a prime qualification for the boards—ceasing to pray the first act in the tragedy of a player's life."

CHAPTER VI.

"AFTER some days of jaunting, feasting, and sporting about among sing-songs, theatres, and concerts, I became a little more reconciled to my lot. One Sunday evening Murray informed me that on the following Monday I must begin my first lessons in my 'profession,' as he called it. I assented, and felt my hopes rise a little; for as yet, sir, I had only seen the scenes from without, and felt fascinated. A few hours among the ropes and pulleys, however, sobered me down.

"The day came round. At the breakfast-table he said to me, 'Now, Zucci, in an hour or so I must know what you are made of; the time for fun is over, the hour for work is come. I look at the boys I train for the stage, on their first arrival, as a merchant does on an unopened bale of goods left at his warehouse. Like him, I unpack them first thing, remove all the stains, such as home-sickness, fear, stupidity, sullenness, and Sunday School touches; I then shake them in the sun, look through them, and count the weak spots, stretch them, to know what they'll stand, and number them. Yes, Zucci, I take every boy's number that comes to me; remember that. From what I have seen of you, although unpacked as yet, I fear you're to turn out a bale of soft goods. However, to-day will settle it; I will unpack you in the back parlour—my warehouse, you know. There I'll number you, shelve you; from thence advertise you among my customers; then, when cut and dried and well shaken together, you'll appear before them on the boards—my counter, you know. If you are of the right stuff, hundreds will receive you, and with their favour make a man of you; if not up to the mark, they'll thrust you from the footlights, as a merchant does a bad shilling out of his change. Now, my boy, get up the steam, and take your finger out of your cheek by the time I return; I mean it this morning, that I do. If out of these limbs of yours I do not bring pence for your purse, brass for your face, and white bread for all the other days of your life, and a feather for my own cap to boot, may I never draw a bow again, or play the man-monkey in the 'Lost Child'—that sublime piece which has put Murray astride on the topmost bough. But more, boy, than all this, I swore to your father, by every drop that splashed on the pavement that night I took you off his hand, I would send you home a gentleman to him; and while I breathe or own the honest name of Murray, I'll keep my word, and a gentleman you shall be.'

"'Mother, let him jump into little Jim's skin-tights; and you, Poll, you see that all is right behind, and the mattresses down. I'll return in ten minutes; I'm only going to Chucklehead's (his name for his barber) to be shaved and see what was up at the 'Vic' last night.'

"So saying, and lighting a silver-mounted pipe, he walked off. His mother rose from the table anything but pleased with her appointment. As she opened the door leading to the upper part of the house, she said, 'You little scrap of human flesh, what are you staring at? You ought to hang a smile on every bit of your body. See Murray's desire to make something of you; and I have just had dropped into my lap an hour's work on your account—a regular hunt through a dozen old boxes for raiment to cover your little bunch of spoiled beef. Laugh, sir, this moment; laugh, and be at home.' This said, she disappeared up-stairs, growling.

"'Poll, you meat-consumer, set about clearing away the breakfast things.' This came down stairs like thunder, making the girl spring up as if a shock of electricity had passed through her limbs. Polly was about sixteen years of age; she had escaped from some reformatory, and had been found by Mr. Murray in some of the theatres selling oranges and lemonade. She was an orphan, and lived with her grandmother in a neighbouring court; she came in the morning, and remained all day, as a domestic servant, and went home at night. She was a strange girl; quick as thought in all her movements; full of nonsense; said droll things to you; seemed to notice everything round about her, form some idea of it, and suddenly come out with her notions of it in such a way as to strike you, making you think, or convulsing you in laughter. When at her work, she wore a spotted frock, with the sleeves cut away; her dark hair was gathered up into two huge tails brought round her head, and fastened in front with a large brass pin, or sometimes simply folded up and tied with a piece of red window-cord. She was what you would call ugly, queer, mischievous, and very droll; yet to the poor fellows under training Polly was always kind after her own style. She worked like a nigger, and made her work pleasant with snatches of song. Her songs were of three classes, she once told me; the names she gave these classes I have never forgot; they were as follows—'Rattlers, 'Weepers,' and 'Heavenlies.' The first she picked up in the streets, the second when in service among gentlefolks, and the third during her stay at the Reformatory; so she told me. She was a good singer; and often when Poll was upstairs and a storm was raging below, she would burst forth with a 'Rattler,' and cause the combatants, against their wills, to turn their rage into a roar of laughter. I have cause to remember

Polly, and will do so, for she was kind, very kind to me.

"After Mrs. Murray had gone up-stairs, and her son to the barber's, Polly dived among the breakfast-dishes, and commenced to wash them; as usual, she cheered her work with a 'Weeper' or 'Rattler.' Suddenly she paused, and, looking me full in the face, she said, 'Zuc, as soon as I am done with my dishes, do you know what I'll do?'

"'How should I know?' I replied.

"'Then I'll tell you. I am just going to make a couple of ear-stoppers. You see there's to be an unpacking to-day.'

"'Whatever do you mean, Polly; and what has that got to do with ear-stoppers?'

"'I mean what I say, Zuc. You're to be unpacked to-day, didn't master tell you? La! how short your memory is to be sure; you'll remember it better after two o'clock to-day, I know—at least little Jim Reed did so.'

"'But still, Polly, about the stoppers?'

"'Well, between master's swearing, fiddling, and the young un's roaring, there's such a row rises that it goes right through my nut, hair and all. I get as flurried as a dog at the Derby. I can't work, I can't sing a 'Rattler,' a 'Weeper,' or a 'Heavenly,' when master's unpacking a little 'un. If I can't get up-stairs I use ear-stoppers now; yet, after all, somehow I have a turn of the shakes on these days.'

"'But what does master do to the boys when unpacking them, Polly?'

"'Why you see, Zuc, when master's on the stage he does all the dancing, leaping, and tom-foolery of the piece, and always requires a little 'un to do some of the parts with him. In teaching them to do this he nearly breaks every bone in their body, so Jim Reed used to tell me. Ay, he told me one day, master used to toss him about like a pancake on Shrove Tuesday, and made him dance to every corner of the room like a rubber ball.'

"'Oh! that's unpacking, Polly?'

"'Ay, that's unpacking, Zucci, and there's more in it than I can tell you; for instance, if you get rusty when he's undoing you, he'll fiddle-bow you all over in grand style, and he hits hard too; so you take my advice, close your ivories and bite your lips, then the screams won't get out, you know; and never forget to lemon-juice your toes, knuckles, and neck; you'll get used to it. We once had a little nigger training, and before being undone every day he put wax out of his ears on his toes, knuckles, and neck. Oh, how that darkey used to laugh at the very thought of splitting master's fiddle-bow. And, oh, how master used to make that darkey dance and spin about to be sure! Missis used to say he could jump through her wedding-ring. But, Zuc, I must run, missis is shutting the boxes, she has found your tights, and the mattresses aint down. When you come out from the parlour, you will find under your pillow a piece of cake and an orange; that's the medicine I give every chap the first day he has his strings cut; it helps him through, you know, Zuc; but if you split on me to missis, I'll serve you out for it, that I will; I'll come and sing a 'Rattler' to your 'Roarer' at the parlour door, and when you come out I won't speak to you. Mind what Poll says to you, if you expect to thrive; now go ahead.'

"Here Poll disappeared into the back-parlour, and commenced to lay down the mattresses, singing in a low, plaintive voice a verse of one of her tenderest 'Weepers.' She had scarcely gone when down came Mrs. Murray with my tights in her hand, her son arriving from the barber's at the same time.

"'Why, aint you dressed, Zucci? time flies!' he exclaimed.

"'The tights have wings too, sir, I've just caught them on the hop; and if you had more time than you needed, it would have been saved had you come and helped me to lime them.'

"This was uttered in a manner so cool that he ventured no reply. He feared her exceedingly, and always obeyed her as quietly and as quickly as Polly did, and as I did after knowing her; from the cat on the rug to the master of the house, all feared, obeyed, and almost hated her. Throwing the tights at me, she ordered me up-stairs, saying, 'and in a twinkling be down, ready for business.' Her manner rendered remonstrance impossible, and delay dangerous. I accordingly obeyed. With a heavy heart, full of sad reflections as to my fate and them that plunged me into it. I arrayed myself in the said tights, consisting of long stockings, drawers, and shirt, of a bright saffron colour. A tear or two stole down my cheek as I looked at myself in showman's dress, and the mysterious speech of Polly did not improve my spirits. I sat down on my bed, thinking on the past and future. I was soon, however, roused from my meditations by the shrill voice of Mrs. Murray; in mock tenderness she called to me, 'Shall I come up and carry you down stairs, or will the darling require his new 'ma to help him into his tights?' This remark caused a feeling to rise in my heart that I did not know was in it before. It rose like a flash of light in a dark place. It was a kind of hardness of heart. I seemed to pass from fear into a kind of careless fury towards my lot, towards Murray, and his mother. When out of their sight it left me, the moment they appeared it returned in full force. The feeling put me in mind of the ways of an old gamecock belonging to a neighbour near our Ragged School; if you approached him with grain he would allow you to stroke him on the back, but if you crawled on your knees and held out your cap to him, his ruff would rise, and he would dash at you with beak and spur. So the conduct of Murray and his mother seemed always to hold out a cap to the eyes of my heart, and it learned to raise its ruff, and use its beak and spur. Ah! sir, living with the wicked hardens the tenderest heart; it makes a little devil of a boy's heart.

"I came down stairs filled with a kind of laughing despair. When I appeared before them, I was welcomed by a shower of bravos from mother and son; she gave me a slap on the back, and said, 'Now, master, you do look like business, thin and straight as an arrow; if Murray do his duty, you'll be able to go through the eye of the ogre in the 'Giant Killer,' without touching a lash of it, by next Christmas.'

"Here Murray rose, saying, 'That he will, mother; come on, Zucci;' and making a few stage bows before me, he pushed open the parlour-door, and said—

'Walk into my pretty parlour,
My pretty little fly.'

"Just before walking in, Poll contrived to catch my eye, she rubbed her fingers over her teeth, as much as to say, 'Keep your ivories shut, Zucci.' I smiled to her, and entered the parlour with Murray, who shut and locked the door behind us."

CHAPTER VII.

"My eye in a moment took in the dimensions and furniture of the mysterious parlour. It was a dingy room, reminding me of what I had heard of those places where, in old times, the law sent murderers to spend their last hours; and if the words 'Condemned Cell' had been written over the top of the door the impression would have been complete. The plaster on the walls was broken, the paper hung in ribbons from them in different parts, the grate was red with rust, as if blood had been poured upon its bars; fragments of broken tobacco-pipes lay all around, interspersed with half-consumed lucifers, and several places were yet damp with recent spitting; a gas-bracket projected over the naked and dusty mantelpiece; the light of day was admitted by a side window, whose glass groaned under the dirt of years, and which made the light to enter the apartment in drab-tinged streams, as they hurried through a broken Venetian blind and a faded curtain; the spiders had triumphed over Polly and her broom, their webs hung in every corner like grey rags; the floor was covered with mattresses to the door. Such was the unpacking-room of the firm of Murray and Mother.

"We now stood face to face; in a moment his coat was in a corner, and his feet enveloped in a pair of old stage shoes; in his hand he flourished an old fiddle-bow. Throwing back his oily curls from his forehead, his eyes twinkled in the drab light of that melancholy room. He gave me a piercing stare, and slowly advanced towards me, grunting between his teeth these words, 'Now, Zucci, for the first step in a gentleman's life, or as York saith—

"A crown, or else a glorious tomb;
A sceptre, or an earthly sepulchre!"'

"I felt sure he intended to do me some bodily harm from his attitude and his words; I raised my arms in defence, and retreated to a corner of the room; seeing this, he growled, 'Down with your hands, you little fiend disguised in boy's skin; down hands, I say, or I'll make your arms hang by your side like a couple of empty jacket sleeves.' Before I knew where I was he had me in his grasp, and I found myself standing on his thigh, while he knelt on the floor with one knee. 'Take your hands from my neck,' he shouted; 'stand as upright as if you were on the floor.' I trembled all over; there was no mistaking the little man now, he meant business; fear and hatred of him prevailed in every corner of my heart as I stood poised on his bony thigh; he gently slipped his hand under one of my feet, saying at the same time, 'Now, you bunch of aspen twigs, prepare for a throw, spread out your hands, and reach the mattress with the silence of an owl on a tombstone.' As if by magic he slipped from under me, and I was sprawling on the mattress in a swimming attitude: I was bathed in sweat from fear and astonishment, but disdained to express either, remembering Polly's advice and the power of the fiddle-bow. He sat laughing at me, and I lay and stared at him. Bringing his face near mine, he pretended to look into my eyes, and said, 'What! not a drop of the crystal? why, man, your shiners will take fire; not one drop yet, eh? Well, you are a brick; you will now be ready for the second move in a twinkling; up, then, and let's try.' My attitude seemed to say 'I won't.' Rising and walking round about me, he put on a face of mock tenderness, and asked, 'Any bones broken, Zucci, dear?' I took no notice. 'Up, boy, a broken bone first throw won't pay, not even for your last ten days' pudding.' A sharp rap with the fiddle-bow brought me to myself and my feet at the same time. We stood at bay once more, he chuckling and giggling, evidently amused at my silent tongue and tearless eyes. Approaching me he said, 'Now, Zucci, spring upon my back, and plant your knees between my shoulders; hold fast as I rise up, seize the cord that runs along the ceiling, cling to it till I cry—free, then spring from my shoulders, clearing my head, and reaching the mattress with open hands.' I looked, but saw not; listened, but heard not. Another application of the bow awoke me to consciousness. He approached me on all fours, grinding between his teeth scraps of curses from old plays; his peculiar attitude, and his rhymed swearing, so frightened me, that as he drew near I sprang between his shoulders as quick as thought; he rose with me thus seated. I then raised myself erect upon his shoulders, and in a moment he cried—'free:' quick as the closing of an eye, he went to the wall and I to the floor. Having struck my face against my fist on reaching the floor, blood rushed from my mouth and nose, covering in its descent the front of my tights. Being a good deal stunned, I lay quiet on the floor; he sat down beside me somewhat concerned till he discovered whence the blood came; he threw some water in my face and put my hands in a basin: we remained in silence on the floor together for some time. At last, turning me on my back, he again expressed some concern in his cold countenance, and muttered to himself—

"'It is not dead midnight.
Cold, fearful drops stand on thy trembling flesh!
What do *I* fear?'"

The sickness left me, and I sat up; he had been meantime constantly passing his hands over all my joints and slightly bending my fingers, as if to discover if any bones were broken. I felt languid in the extreme; and, like a person newly out of sleep, I stared listlessly around me. He was deadly pale, the veins across his brow were swollen and its furrows filled with sweat, but in his face not a muscle moved; like white marble soiled was that face; yea, like a dial behind which moves no wheels. Affections human behind that face there were none. He loved no creature on God's world but his own wretched little self; often has he pushed me aside, saying, as he passed, 'My name is Murray, and let no dog bark when I speak; aside, Milksops all, was not the world made for *me* to bustle in?' He seemed much relieved, however, by my sitting up, wiped my face and hands with a sponge, and smoothed my hair with his own pocket-comb. Taking off his slippers and putting on his coat, he informed me that my first lesson was over. Dropping a shilling between my shirt and chest he took me by the hand, saying—

"''Tis not enough to help the feeble up,
But to support him after; fare you well;'"

and left me.

"As I came from the parlour Mrs. Murray and Polly were busy cleaning some dish-covers; they both stared at me; Mrs. Murray said, in a mock tender voice, 'So, my boy, without breaking your neck you've got over the first stone in the path of a gentlemen, eh? Ah, child (eyeing the blood on my clothes), you'll have your reward; showers of buns and bon-bons from the youngsters in the pit, bouquets from the boxes, and bravos in thunder-claps from the galleries at your first pant. (pantomime) next Christmas; that will pay you for everything, heal all your scratches, wipe the sweat from your brow, and make you burst your tights with delight. La! you *do* have a handful of bright days before you; aint he, Polly?'

"'I'm sure of that, missis,' said Polly; 'he doesn't

know he's born yet; but he's a brick, hasn't squeaked once, although the claret (blood) has been tapped, and the chalk a flying (paleness). La! missis, if he dance a polka with the iron breeches on as quietly, won't he be a stunner; make master's fortune in no time, and himself a man before he's out of long clothes?'

"Here a significant look from missis changed the conversation. I knew not the reason, but resolved to quiz Polly the first opportunity. Poll remained silent for some time, and all at once commenced singing in a soft, plaintive voice, a verse of one of her best 'weepers;' here it is:—

'I never knew a mother's love
 Yet happy were my days;
For by my own dear father's side
 I sang my simple lays.
He died, and heartless strangers came,
 Ere closed o'er him the grave;
They tore me weeping from his side,
 And claimed me as their slave.'

"While she was singing I crawled up stairs, and found under my pillow a couple of oranges and a piece of pudding. Polly, the boy's friend, put them there. To me that girl was a puzzle and a mystery; she was always crossing your path in some new light, and some new feature of her character was coming into view when least expected. Having escaped from my tights I sauntered out for a walk, rejoicing in my freedom and also that my first lesson was over. But such meetings so often took place, and lessons such as I have described were so frequently repeated, that I began positively to take pleasure in what at first made my bones ache with pain, and my heart strings tremble with fear. After a few weeks' training in this way I could pass with ease through the eye, in at the mouth, and down the nose of huge faces sketched on paper and stretched on frames. I became an adept in my profession; I was praised and petted by the whole household, until pride and conceit, like a couple of ugly warts, grew on my character; and before they were removed many a cuff and kick from God and man they cost me—nay, even now, sir, I feel their roots shooting and growing within me.

"Time wore on, and I continued to please and excel in feats of agility, not forgetting to annoy them with occasional outbursts of self-will and conceit; sometimes I was even pettish to Polly; she took it quietly; but what she did not like she had the knack of most faithfully remembering, and in her own way most effectually revenging. Her memory was one of her most remarkable faculties; whatever was committed to its care was faithfully reproduced to the very letter. From what follows you will see Polly thought that the time for applying the damper had come. One night at supper I happened to make free with Miss Polly's work, and unintentionally brought her into trouble, out of which it cost her something to wriggle. As we were lighting our candles to retire to bed she gently tapped me on the shoulder, and whispered in my ear, 'Zucci, dear, every dog has 'im's day; smoke that, darling; and may you and the fleas have a lively night of it.' So saying she turned to collect her supper-things, and to make some preparations for the morrow's breakfast, aiding her work with a verse from one of her Irish 'rattlers.'

> ''Twas at the Pig and Cat
> Where Judy met her Pat,
> With his big nose so red;
> Oh! says she, *you're untrue*,
> And troth I'll punish you;
> And then she broke his head.
> Her brother Ted was standing by,
> Who nately black'd her father's eye;
> For he was bold and frisky.'

This sent Murray and Mother to bed convulsed in laughter. That 'rattler' and Poll's whisper informed me a storm was brewing, and I guessed on whose head it would fall. I accordingly ascended to bed, sorry at heart I had offended a friend so really true as poor Polly. After breakfast next morning Murray and his Mother went out, leaving me to pick the spangles off an old stage dress previous to their being put on another; and Polly was busy with household work. All went on quietly for a little, till Poll, unable to resist the opportunity of punishing me for last night's work, said, 'Well, Master Zuc, I didn't much like the sauce and sour apples you put on my plate last night. You're going on anyhow now since you've got over your unpacking, jest like a ball thrown among a lot o' ninepins; you hit one, and make it knock the heads of all the others together; but jest let me tell you, Poll's not to be knocked over when it pleases YOU; if I run to one side you may come smack agen the wall—that'll make the chips flee out of you, though you were made o' London Bridge pavement.'

"'But Poll, I said, it was only in fun; I didn't do it to hurt you—never; you've been too kind to me since I came here; I thought you could take a joke.'

"'Knocking missis' head and mine together,' she said, 'that's no joke; we strike fire, and then there's smoke in the house. Once *her* tongue's let loose on a poor cove, it's like standing in the way of a cartful of stones poured down a hill, every one jumps and bounds, and hits you jolly hard; so her words, unless your nut were made of oak, and your heart of iron, would knock you into a jelly. I was too rum a gal at the reformatory, or I might have got a good place out of it, and I am too far under missis' thumb *now*, or I'd bolt from the lot of ye; were it not for some things I'd hook it this morning.'

"'What things, Poll?'

"She replied, 'There's my grandmother, poor old soul, she lives on my few shillings, they keep her out of the workhouse; besides, when I was a rum un she always took my part, and, in the teeth of them all, she declared I would mend; *that*, *Zuc*, keeps me from bolting. This morning, all through your fun last night, missis has nearly torn me to pieces—casting all my old larks in my face; la! am sure her words flew about my ears like the knives of the Chinese conjurer about the head of his mate; had he moved an inch they would have stuck in it like pins in a cushion. So do missis' words if you stay to think of them. But I never moves; she doesn't know my soft place yet—she never knew it; God and grannie know IT. If SHE did she would very soon make it as hard as the street; I'm always game before her; if SHE saw the white feather among my hair, the sooner the undertaker has my measure the better for me. Our missis is jest like old Isaac the hawker's basket, you'll get out of it anything you like, *except* what you want. She's as free of kindness as his basket is of the genuine article.'

"'But, Poll, I'm truly sorry I've caused you so much trouble. You'll forgive me for this time, won't ye? I'll not hold my head so high again.'

"Looking me full in the face, she said, softly and seriously, 'THIS time I will, but don't you try it on AGAIN, if you please. You can't do very well without ME in this house; you're only head and shoulders out of the egg yet. Stick to me, Zucci; I don't want a rise out of ye, but only I likes to help the chicks till they can use their wings, and to put 'em up to all the dodges o' the place to save their bacon. Murray'll stick to ye, too, but jest as the butcher does to a pig, for what he'll get out of it. And, besides, Zuc, you haven't had on your breeches yet; how you're to get into them or out of them I know not, but I often ask—How? when they're making all the pretty things in the world of ye, and you as open to their nonsense as a gravel walk, or a sandbank is to water.'

"I said, 'Whatever do you mean, Polly, by these said breeches? I saw some winks and looks pass between missis and you when they were mentioned one day before. There's a good girl, do let me into the secret; will you?'

"She answered, 'If you wanted a rod to go round a corner, and the only one you had were straight, what would you do with it? Make it crooked, of course. If you had a knee which, as it was made at first, could not move in a certain way, yet in that very way you had to go ahead, what would you do with it? Of course alter it to answer the purpose; that's clear, Zucci. Well, up in that box there is an iron thing which gives the knee the new style; it's the very shape of the knee, it's lined with wool, and has several screws which master knows how to turn. After a few turns, the little bone on the top of the knee, about the size of a penny, is pushed down out of its place. After it's all over the coves tell me their legs go like steam. But don't it make the squeakers chase each other up your throat! I calls 'em the knee-breeches. You aint considered a man neither, no not even worth your meat, till you have been breeched. Like to see them, Zuc?'

"While in the act of taking down the box, the knocker announced some one at the door. Poll rushed to her dusting and sweeping, and I became busy at my spangle-picking. Poll, as usual, took refuge among the lines of a song, and went to the door singing—

'I'm a laughing Zingarella;
  Fear not that an evil eye
Ever lurks amid the glances
  That I give while passing by;
For my heart is free and joyous
  As a wild bird on the wing,
And kind smiles of welcome greet me
  When I dance and gaily sing.'

"After dinner I watched an opportunity and slipped out. The iron breeches and the pain they would cause filled me with such fears that I resolved to run away. Where my parents were I knew not, and to them, therefore, I could not fly. My 'handful of bright days' vanished, and all my dreams of becoming a great actor melted into nothing, just like one's breath in the air on a frosty morning. I was almost broken-hearted, like the traveller in the desert, having the cup of cold water dashed from his scorching lips in the moment of drinking; pain past was about to be renewed, only altered in form, and the period of its duration was hid from me by a space and time unlimited; I was like the two schoolboys who set out one day to discover the spot on which the limbs of the rainbow rested, believing the story that if they found it there would be a pair of silver slippers awaiting them. Over hill and dale they wandered; the bow as they approached seemed to rise higher and higher among the cliffs, it continued to flee and they to pursue, till night swallowed up the bow, and they were lost. So my bright prospects continued to vanish; darkness blotted out my bow, a wicked hand had also removed my silver slippers. My hopes sank in my heart like stones to the bottom of a pool. In this spirit I wandered along the Brixton Road; weary and sad I sat down on a heap of building materials, and stared at the fading light of the setting sun; I remained near the spot till it became quite dark, and the moon began to rise behind the chimney-tops of the distant village. On leaving the spot I wandered through an old deserted garden, partly cleared for building purposes; a portion of the fence still stood, and at an entrance of one of the walks was an arch, surmounted by a wooden soldier with outstretched arms and a sword in each hand, which, catching the evening breeze, made him wheel and beat the air. 'That's me,' I said, 'pulled and tossed about by every one, as this man of wood is by every wind that blows; like him, I strike right and left, but touch nothing—make no impression; continually grinding the air, but producing neither chaff nor flour—nothing.' As I passed from under the arch, at the bottom of the walk stood an old walnut tree; I sat down at its root and stared in the direction of the wooden soldier; the moonlight was not sufficiently abundant to make him visible, but as the wind flew over him I could distinctly hear the burr of his old rusty pivot as he hewed it in its flight. I could not help saying, 'Some day the hand of the builder will take you down, old boy; perhaps a better berth is awaiting you, and the wind and you may fight it out another day among sweeter flowers, and in a garden that's not deserted; such gardens there are; all that's wanted is the hand to take you down and put you up. I am like you; I am fixed; I can't escape the iron breeches; in them I must fight, and in that dingy room too, till the hand come that is to put me up or take me down. Whose hand shall it be? WHEN shall it be? O Lord, how long?' On that night, in the deserted garden, at the root of the old walnut tree, talking to the wooden soldier on the arch, I got my first *real* glimpse of a Father in heaven. While thus employed, a number of labourers, returning from work, passed near where I was sitting, and to lighten their homeward journey were singing a snatch of that well-known song—

'There's a good time coming, boys,
Wait a little longer.'

"These words seemed to fall from heaven on my heart; had they *really* done so a deeper impression could not have been made. They seemed to fill up a gap in my very soul. These working men neither knew nor saw me. The following questions rose to my tongue. 'How should I be here to listen? What could make them sing the very words my soul needed?' Something within me responded 'Tush boy, 'tis not man—it's the finger of God.' As the hungry eagle clutcheth at its prey, refuseth to let it go, and carrieth it home with her, so did my soul clutch that snatch of song; for days, for weeks, it was its meat and drink, and ever since that hour a faint impression of the presence of God in my affairs remained on my spirit. From that day until the day he was pleased to reveal his Son in me, the impression of that night never left my mind. It was anything but clear, anything but scriptural; nevertheless, I can't help thinking it was the first drop of that shower of the water of life which long after blessed my weary soul. But, sir, were it not for the Spirit of God and the Scriptures, how foggy would man's religion be! For instance, after this night I continually felt as if some Great Being was a witness of, and took an interest in, my affairs; although I saw no fixed form, he moved beside me, as if wrapped in a large mantle. So vividly did I feel this that I thought I heard the very rustle of his garments; so convinced in my own mind was I that he was real, that I talked to him, complained to him, referred to him, prayed to him. I have learned since that pious people call such feelings natural religion—not true religion; in all the feelings of true religion there is a constant reference to the blood of Jesus. I afterwards came to know, that without the shedding of blood there was no forgiveness. Precious blood, thou makest the foulest clean! While such thoughts were passing through my mind the church clock struck eight. I resolved to return home. I felt more cheerful, and dashed from my mind all my plans of escape, and mused, as I returned, on the good time coming, and resolved to wait a little longer. I could have put on the iron breeches that very night, and allowed the two penny-shaped bones to be pushed ever so far down, even to the place appointed them by the most particular ballet master in London.

CHAPTER VIII.

"When I reached home Polly was standing at the head of the street; on seeing me she rushed up and laid her hand on my shoulder, exclaiming, 'Zucci! wherever have you been? There's smoke in the house everywhere but in the chimney; you've lit a regular flamer in all corners of it. I could light my morning fire with the handle of the pump in the washhouse even. Missis is rambling all over the place anyhow, jest as if her head was in a bag. There's a chair tumbling here, a jug there, and sure you could light your bedroom candle at any one of her eyes. Sometimes she swears, at other times she runs over all her doings for you—missing out the bad 'uns. Yes, Zuc, if I mistake not, she was once praying for you. La!

missis is up to something when SHE comes the length of praying; she sometimes cries out, "He's drowned." Here Murray strikes in, and cries, "Drowned, yes, he's drowned—by this time he has become a drop in the ocean of London prigs." Missis gives him a backer in words that cut like knives; they come hot and sharp right off the point of her tongue; all of 'em cut him into the bone, I know, from the faces he makes, but he says nothing. Then he blows her up for not putting the butter on thick enough; again, she blows him down with regular hard 'uns, from the very pit of her stomach. La! then it all ends in "What shall we say to Footy and his wife about their kid?" Now, Zuc, if you havn't brass enough, melt all your buttons, and stick it over your soft places. I'll bolt, and say you're coming as tired as a coster's donkey from the fair: game to the heel now Zuc.' After uttering the above speech as fast as her tongue could move, and in a most excited manner, she disappeared. I followed her. On entering, such a scene! Missis, choking with rage, fell to howling at me; master, walking up and down like a stage king, spoke as slowly as if in the murder-scene of a play, stared at me, pointed at me with his finger, enumerated all he had done for me, and finished by saying, 'Now, my little bit of floating capital, repeat this again, and I'll walk you to the door; that will form the last passage in the piece: explain yourself; account for your conduct.'

"I simply replied I had strayed too far before I was aware of it, and told him where I had been. He smiled mockingly; missis groaned out, 'Tell that to the marines;' and Polly finished up by saying, 'La! missis, I always told you the young 'un had a bee in his cap.' In my inmost soul, where no ear heard me, I sung, 'There's a good time coming, Zuc, just wait a little longer.' I took some supper, and disappeared up-stairs for the night.

"After the storm had blown over, and everything had found its right place again, I had no cause to regret it. It seemed to teach them I was not to be dealt with as a thing, but as a human being; or, if not, that I was a thing with a human soul in it—at least a heart with some feelings in it. I received more consideration from all parties; occasionally, now, I would hear of my parents, and sometimes even a present from them would reach me.

"The autumn quarter was approaching, or, in their language, the 'season' was at hand; sundry additions were made to the furniture, all the bed-clothes were washed; the parlour, or rather the 'condemned cell,' was re-papered, the mattresses well switched and aired, coals for the winter were laid in; the whole establishment underwent a complete change—at least on the surface. One day I got orders to turn out all the dresses, foils, wigs, and masks; repairing, burnishing, combing, and colouring, were the duties laid to every hand in the place. Poll used to call it 'Murray's hay-season.' 'If anything go wrong now,' she would say, 'we will require opera-glasses to count the plums in the pudding, and there will be so little skyey in the bottle, that missis will fall to pieces with the dry rot; and, if we be not as busy as fleas in an Irishman's collar, we will have to hang like bats in a chimney all winter.' She herself went tearing through her work as if she were mad, making the house ring with an Irish 'rattler;' or, if the task on hand was of a quiet nature, she would sweeten it by gently singing one of her tenderest 'weepers,' and very rarely, but sometimes it would happen, an incident would send her thoughts back to her stay at the Reformatory, then we would on such occasions get a snatch of a 'heavenly' by way of a change. I never shall forget one such occasion. The work on hand was of a quiet nature; the whole house was present. Poll burst forth in the following verse, her eyes shining, her hands resting on her knees, and her countenance full in the sun:—

> 'What am I, O thou glorious God,
> And what my father's house to thee,
> That thou such mercies hast bestowed
> On ME, the vilest reptile, ME!
> I take the blessing from above,
> And wonder at thy boundless love.'

We all became quiet; every one somehow was awed, and none of us more so than missis; she reminded me of a child who hears a peal of thunder, and hides its head in its mother's breast, remaining quiet till it's over, then looking up with caution and by degrees.

Master's teeth and lips seemed glued together. Poor Poll began again with her little brush to polish her buckles and small brass ornaments as if nothing had happened. Murray and Mother knew enough of God to torment them when they dared to think. Of Polly's feelings, except on occasions like these, concerning divine things, I could never make anything; her natural element seemed to be working, singing, joking, raising storms of laughter by her quaint old world-sayings, and doing little kind things quietly. She had power, Polly. Power over us all; none of us cared for rousing her, or making her our enemy. Even missis, when angry with her, would not rashly trample on her toes, and sometimes even swallowed her anger, simply saying under her breath she was a 'necessary evil—a she-devil.' When they did quarrel it was awful.

"As the 'season' drew nearer, master had a good many visitors, principally on business. Among them were ballet-girls, not a few, arranging with him for instruction in their art, in prospect of the winter. Oh, sir, the miseries of these poor women! Their scanty clothing, little money, and personal sufferings! God, their own souls, and such men as Murray, only know the price they pay to be allowed to pick up their crust off the boards. Ill-paid, ill-fed, ill-clad, and ill-used, is every one of them. If gentlefolks only knew what one night's amusement, which only costs them a few shillings, costs these 'white slaves,' it would turn their hair grey; theirs truly is a dance of death; yet they become accustomed to it—seldom leave it till they die off or are ruined.

"Murray was considered a first-class dancer, and, consequently, while the 'season' lasted, was frequently employed as a teacher of his art during the day, and as frequently in the evening as a performer among second-rate theatres. During this portion of the year the 'Cell' from morning till evening was never empty; but, like every other 'Condemned Cell,' its history should be but sparingly told, and but rarely, if ever, written. What has passed before my eyes in that 'chamber of horrors' I could not, dare not, shall not pour into the ear of any human being! Among its visitors, however, there was one of whom I should like to say a few words—Miss Mary Drew. She was the only child of a retired physician, and lived in one of the neighbouring squares. Her connexion with the Murrays was so remarkable I cannot resist giving you some account of it. Among the Murrays she went by the name of 'Miss Mary,' or 'the Spectre'—her surname was never mentioned. From the following simple incident, however, I was unintentionally introduced to her, but for a moment, and yet in that brief space I formed the acquaintance of one of the most holy, eccentric, and melancholy, of all my lady friends; but as a friend she was one of the most steady, sagacious, and daring—anything the object of her friendship required was procured at all hazards to herself.

"Before I proceed further I may mention she was named 'the Spectre' from the nature of her visits; they were short, and full of warning. From that lady's lips, twice a year at least, Murray and Mother were taught the plan of salvation, and the awful nature, nay the certain destruction to soul and body of a life of sin.

"One day while in the 'Cell' acquiring some peculiar steps in a dance, previous to starting for the country with Murray, his mother opened the door, and hurriedly announced Miss Mary. At the mention of her name, something like emotion suddenly passed over his countenance, and as quickly disappeared, leaving as little trace behind as does the shadow of the summer cloud when it glides over the waving grain.

"She was attired in a dark striped silk gown, fitting closely round the neck, with a plain linen collar, fastened by a small brooch; on her wrists she wore linen cuffs, beautifully embroïdered; her bonnet was neat but exceedingly plain, tied under her chin with a broad green ribbon, a couple of daisies held together by two stems of grass, its only decoration; she was tall and handsome in person, and exceedingly rapid in all her movements. Her hair was as dark as the raven's wing, and disposed in braids over a fine white forehead, across which ran three slight furrows, which men who write books call lines of thought. Her eyes were large and of a deep dark-brown colour; when she looked at you their expression was soft and melancholy in the extreme, but if excited or offended these same melancholy eyes would sparkle, burn, nay, turn into flames, her words the meanwhile piercing the offender's very heart like daggers. Her countenance was round, the features regular, but strongly marked. When engaged in any work of mercy, her face, particularly her eyes, looked absolutely beautiful. Sometimes she would sit down and clasp her long white fingers in each other, and lay her hands on her knee;—at such a moment her spirit seemed to wander far away. At other times, in the same attitude, her countenance would express nothing but anguish, then stray tears, bright as bits of her own eyes, would roll down her cheeks. Whilst in these moods, if any one approached her, she would quickly brush away the tears, become collected in a moment, and fully engage herself in whatever was on hand. On the day in question, as she entered, Murray seemed struck with the paleness of her countenance and exclaimed:—

'What! Miss Mary, still among the tombs! You ladies are frail, ay, as the glasses where you view yourselves, which are as easy broke as they make forms.'

"'Yes, Murray,' she retorted, her eyes gleaming, ''tis safer to be THAT which we destroy, than by destruction dwell in doubtful joy.'

"'Come, Mary,' said Murray, 'priestly sayings and pulpit phrases are edged like chisels, and when flung are sure to wound the breast that meets them.'

"'But, Murray,' she replied, softly, yet firmly, "'when the tool-chest is open, all temptation to the use of the chisel should be avoided.'

"'Right, Mary, right, we'll close the chest and dance on its lid instead,' responded Murray, and endeavoured to change the current of her thoughts by making inquiries about her father, and the friends he and she had just left in the country. Again, unintentionally, however, he opened the same vein of thought by asking her the following question:—

"'What made you look so sad when you came in?'

"She turned herself round, and looking him full in the face said, 'Sir, by accident my mind's eye fell on a scene of the past, and, like a young horse, my spirit shied, being frightened; surely a woman alarmed may shed a tear without having to write a volume to account for it.'

"O sir, would that every one that ever pined under Murray's petty tyranny had seen him at that moment. How crest fallen! Little at any time, but how much less just then! In my own soul I whispered, 'How now, master nimble-toes, there's a step for *you*, quite new too, and not from France either.' I admired the lady, but, sir, how my soul scorned the man—that awfully little man, which for the time I was obliged to call master! How the little thing did move about; with the silence of a shadow it paced the floor of the 'Cell!' Murray's eye lost its power, his tongue its scraps of old plays and stage wit, and his brow its brass; after these deductions there remained one of the commonest faces among men—a child might have pulled his chin with impunity.

"But, as a man recovering from a stunning blow in a contest, with what little strength is left once more shows fight, so did he, and once more renewed it by saying, 'Miss Mary! the recollections of the past seem to fall like sparks of fire among your heart-strings, and to make your tongue like pointed steel. Let the past be buried; see that you shape well the present, and leave the future to God.'

"'Murray,' here rising to her full height, and in a calm and mournful voice, she replied, 'the past is buried here (pointing to her breast), and it is buried yonder (looking to the sky) among the leaves of the book of God's remembrance. If the blood of Jesus has not flowed over those pages where our past is written, better you and I had been buried before that part of our history we call past had existed. In the past I was a boarding-school fool, 'pleased with a rattle, and tickled with a straw.' Then I was confiding, and you were designing; I was shielded then by a hand at that time by me unseen. You were baulked by a power unknown, and to you still unknown; that hand was his who laid down his life for me ere I was born; that power that restrained you is the same that keeps the sea within its bounds, and which will miserably destroy all who love not the Lord Jesus. The present is yours. May his Spirit so 'shape it' as to lead you to the foot of the cross—there, there is forgiveness and a happy present, beyond it is a future so transcendantly glorious that they who can call it their own—like the Maker of it—despise the shame attached to a holy life on earth, yea, for the joy that is set before them, cheerfully endure mockings and scourgings, bonds and imprisonments; are willing to be stoned or sawn asunder, tempted or slain, and to finish their journey here destitute, afflicted, and tormented. Oh, Murray, turn and flee. I say, Murray, flee while it is day, "the night cometh wherein no man can work,"

"Jesus ready stands to save you,
Full of pity, love, and power."

Much that we dream not of in our future will have become the past in your life and mine in the months that must intervene before we meet again. Murray, perhaps ETERNITY may enclose us both in its awfully sublime realities ere we meet again; each click of the old dusty clock out there announces to the attentive ear the flight of a host of souls to their last doom. Murray, eternity without Christ is—hell! Eternity with Christ is—heaven! See to it; NOW is the accepted time, to-morrow may become NEVER! an everlasting NEVER!!'

"Her face streaming with tears, she bowed herself to the door and disappeared. Murray sat in a corner for a moment, his faced buried in his hands; he was speaking to himself; all I heard was, 'Yes, the hour is past NOW—go, noble, generous soul, God *alone* deserves you.' Here he started up, and for the first time during the interview had become conscious of my presence—painfully conscious! He was troubled. At last he called me to him, and said, 'Zuc, give me your hand; look at me; if EVER you reveal at home or abroad what you have witnessed this day it will cost you your life.' Flinging my hand from him, he said, 'Remember my words,' and passed out at the door.

"Murray's threat; Mary's awful warning; that sermon on salvation, death, judgment, and eternity, delivered in a voice so musical, yet melancholy, kept ringing in my ears, and her majestic appearance kept floating before my eyes till I became bewildered. I, too, called her 'the Spectre,' and trembled all over, I almost believed I had been in the world of spirits. But soon was I recalled to the world of mortals, for scarcely had Murray joined his mother (who had also been warned by Mary) in the front parlour than words ran high. In their words, however, there was no—gospel. I crept in while the following conversation was passing between Murray and mother. Murray was standing like a statue of flesh, in the middle of the floor.

"'Too fine for the foot-lights, boy—too straight in the back for the green-room. No, no boy, all men in some part of their voyage through life have to pitch over-board the jewel-box, and cling to the pea-jacket and brass buttons. Your time came early; it is high time to cease staring into the sea, and biting your fingers for what you've done. Let it drop astern, and turn your face to the weather; finish your voyage like a man; forget the past, become jolly in the present; trust your present crew, my boy—many have come to shore with a worse, and very few have finished their voyage with one so good.'

"During this unfeeling speech on the part of his mother, Murray, who evidently had been thinking of what had passed in the 'Cell,' when she became silent, started; fixing his eyes upon the ceiling, and turning his back on his mother, he exclaimed—

'"Oh, stay!—I have no power to let her pass;
My hand would free her, but my heart says—no.
As plays the sun upon the glassy streams,
Twinkling another counterfeited beam,
So seems this gorgeous beauty to mine eyes;
Fain would I woo her, yet I dare not speak."'

"Scarcely had he finished the quotation than his mother shouted, 'Murray, you're a little fool!' Then, said the son, 'you're a double one; for not only are you a little one, but you're also an old one, and one without feeling; your heart's as hard as a cobbler's lapstone, on which have been beaten the shoe-soles of three generations. Poll, my candle.' The subject of singular feelings, and the victim of remorse, he retired to bed, but not to sleep, I'm certain. The mother, sore vexed, also retired to her room to 'nurse her wrath to keep it warm;' on no occasion did she ever say—Die. I followed. So ended that eventful day.

"The scene with Mary never left my mind. Was she a female missionary? she had all the piety necessary for one. Her rank, her education said she was not. That period in the past, at the sight of which 'her spirit shied like a young horse,' said she was not. The little man's familiarity towards one so infinitely his superior in every way seemed to point to another kind of relationship. What could it be?—that was the question with me. I resolved to sound Polly on the subject. A few days after I was appointed to assist her in some work connected with some of Murray's performances. Being a good deal alone with Polly, I broke the ice on the vexed question as follows:—

"'I say, Poll, stop that 'rattler,' and answer me a few questions—there's a good girl.'

"She replied, 'Master Zuc, keep your compliments till Poll asks them—never pay for what you haven't got; la! I did think you had grown wiser by this time, than fry fish before you've caught 'em—you *are* a muff. I see, Zuc, master will have to break fifty bows over your head before he puts 'nouse' in it.'

"'Ah, Poll, I can see you know what I'm after,' I replied.

"'In course I do; you carry your idears in a gauze bag—a person with one eye could measure 'em and count 'em too; ye're jest on the fidgets to know who Miss Mary is, aint ye? Don't look 'mazed,' for I'm a witch for a guesser.'

"'Well, Polly, do you know her?'

"'Know her, Zuc? Know the darling? Ay, Zuc, and love her too. She's put her white hand on my black nut too often for me to forget one of the best of God's creatures. If you but heard her talk of Christ, Zuc, you would not forget neither; and when she's a-doin of it, too, she looks at you so straight, so soft, and her eyes get so full of Jesus that they run over. I often think I see little pictures of Him in the tears as they chase each other down her cheek; and her hand, too, it's never still all the time she's speaking of Christ to ye—it's either on your shoulder, or patting your cheek, or smoothing your hair. I do believe, Zuc, there's not a bone in all that little white hand of Miss Mary's—I'm sure there aint.'

"I asked, 'But, Polly, how did she come to know the Murrays?'

"'Zuc, do ye know what a hedgehog does when a dog's a-mouthin of him? he curls himself up to hide his soft parts; so do I. Take your answer out of that.'

"'Polly, did ever I split on you in anything you ever trusted me with? I never did, and I never will. Honour me this time also—I would you.'

"Here she burst into one of her wild songs; the work went on, and I became silent. After a considerable pause she went to the window, then to the door, and looked out. After shutting it with care, and walking round the room once or twice, she came to a stand in the middle of the floor. What a figure!

Her black hair disposed of in two coarsely-plaited tails, tied together by a piece of red window-cord; her frock sleeves cut away close up to the shoulder, revealing a couple of fat arms as red as lobsters; her countenance was as solemn, and almost as grim, as one you see carved in stone over the arch of a cathedral door. 'Zuc, look up,' were the first words she uttered. I did so. Spitting on the palm of her hand, she commanded me to do the same, and I obeyed. 'Now,' she said, 'lay yours in mine.' I did so; she grasped it firmly, and held it out from her at arm's-length, nearly level with our faces. We stood for a moment like a couple of combatants crossing swords at the commencement of a fray. Beholding me for a moment, her eyes, like lighted candles, seemed to search every nook and corner of my heart. At last she said, 'If I tell you, will ever you split upon me?' I replied, 'Never, never, Polly.' Here increasing the firmness of her grasp, she replied, making long pauses between her words, 'If you do, may you never have a true mate at your elbow when you're roughing it! may this hand I hold grow as stiff as the leg of a coster's barrow! and may your tongue never move again, except when you've a sorrow to tell!' 'Agreed, agreed,' I cried. She let go my hand, and we each resumed our seats.

"'What I'm about to tell you, Zucci, is what Murray's mother calls a family secret; very few of their friends know, and they that do don't live here about. The people that come to the house now only see her, as you have, once or twice a year, and call her 'the Spectre;' but why she comes, and how she became acquainted with the Murrays, is not known to any of them.'

"'But, Polly, why keep it such a secret?' I asked; 'they might be proud of her acquaintance.'

"'When you hear all about it, I suppose that will answer your question, master Zuc. If missis did not need to hide it, catch her keep it to herself; you are a 'mooney' to live longer with Murray and Mother than one round of the clock, and not know that anything that would swell out their cheeks would never be swallowed; catch 'em! THEY make face all that will be face; la! am sure, when she's three sheets in the wind, how she does talk about her rich relations and their doins; and how, out of pure love, she married a poor feller, and was sent to the door-step by 'em all for the doin of it; and how, for her poor feller's sake, she had to fight as many battles with her friends and foes as had Othello. Haven't you seen her go smack down upon her knees and confess her sins and her greatness, and then rise up and go it on the floor there like Bob Orton's peacock, with his tail spread in the sun as he walks round the mews up there. La! if Miss Mary had been a relation, pity our 'sounders' (ears), there would have been the noise of a church bell in each of them; nay, Zucci, but because neither the little man nor she could suck her in and make her a relation, because they made a mess of it when they did try, it's that which makes the old lady mum. Her fingers are sore burned when she sings out; she never says—Die. No, Zucci, they *did* make a muddle of it, or, as Miss Mary has it, "a loving, holy, sleepless God ordained it otherwise." No, Zucci, Miss Mary's God would not have it nohow. Now, Zuc, are you ready for the rest of it?'

"'Oh, yes, Polly, do go on—you *do* tell a tale well,' I replied.

"'I don't want your butter, Zucci; only your ears.' This she said, alluding to my small compliment; to her praise was hateful. 'Well,' she resumed, 'the whole affair took place shortly before Murray joined the theatre, and but a short time before I entered their service. In the evenings—while I was at work, and believing I was green and not taking notice—they used to talk about the whole affair. And how the little man did suffer during the first week or two! His eyes seemed frightened at his nose, for they sunk as far back from it as they could get; his face was as white as a sheet, and he would neither eat, nor sleep, nor do anything. He went on anyhow; he would not look out at the door; he quarrelled with the sun, moon, and stars, as if they had no right to shine when he wished to go out—pretty little dear! Had he been tall enough and strong enough he would have taken the kitchen-broom and swept them all out of the sky. How these poor suns, moons, and stars did suffer, to be sure, while he was ill; he called them everything—but stars. That he would not do. Ay, Zucci, and these same stars nearly cost me my life too; for one night he and his mother were nasty to me, so while the little man was a-walkin the floor, repeating bits of plays, 'bauncing the moon,' and snapping at me, my powder caught fire, and, laying down the plate I was washing, I looked at him, and sang—

"Twinkle, twinkle, little star;
How I wonder what you are!
Up above the world so high,
Like a diamond in the sky."

How his eyes did twinkle! in a twinkle he was round the table after me, and in less than a twinkle I was out at the door; didn't I foot it up the court to granny's! as fast as if all the twinkling stars in the sky had been bowling at my heels! Missis came to granny's next morning and made it up, and I went back; ever after that they talked about everything before me just as if I was one of the chairs or tables; understand, Zuc, as if I had neither 'shiners' nor 'sounders.' One part of the bargain I do remember; she was to be to me a mother, and I was to be to her a daughter. My eye, such a pair! We did love each other! when she played at mother, it was generally on scrubbing-days, and being my mother, she had a right to get out of me all she could without extras. One day she came it so strong that I turned all at once—daughter. I was so naughty as to speak back. All the forenoon I'd been scrubbing jest like a nigger, and yet she grumbled and spoke about taking her love from me. I jumped to my pins and said—"Mother, your love lies so near your teeth that if you open your mouth much wider it will fall into my pail and get drownded! keep it down there, pointing to her breast, and it'll neither be heard nor seen, for in you that place is so deep, the well in the yard's nothing to it; I'm tired being your daughter! there's no love in you to me or no one: jest as Betty Huggins cut all her hair out, and flung it into Pat's coffin as they were a-screwin it down, and went about some days with a naked nut, so you buried all your love in the poor fellow's coffin you call Murray's father—him you married for love, and got the sack from all your rich relations for a-doin of it! Yes, mother; if you ever had love in you, its where Betty Huggins's hair is—in your husband's grave! I've seen none of it, nor has anyone who knows you; I'll be your daughter no longer! so, mother, good-bye," and off to granny I came. She came after me once more. Once more we made it up, and we both agreed to play at mother and daughter no more. Since that I'm let alone to do my bit in my own way.'

"'But, Polly, you have forgot Miss Mary,' I hinted in the most gentle way.

„'Indeed, Master Zuc! I'll be cold—ay, as cold as a lamp-post in November, when I forget Miss Mary.

But you've forgot your manners, sir; when you ask a gal to tell you anything, she must do it in her own style—so this is my style.'

"'I beg pardon, Polly,' I replied, 'I want it in your own style; I like your style.'

"Well, after giving me a quiet snub for again using a little butter, she began by saying, 'Well, Murray got better, made it up with the sun, moon, and stars, took to his grub, and went to work on the boards like a good 'un, and as if nothing had happened.'

"'How easily he gets over things, Polly, compared with other men; some would have drowned or hanged themselves for less,' I remarked. 'Was it a love affair?'

"'Yes,' she replied, 'a red-hot affair. So would he have drowned himself, but he's mighty afeard of the other world; won't face it anyhow; something in it always gives him the shivers; when he's ill any time, he is such a coward he upsets the whole house—some one must always be with him; and he's always asking if they think he'll get better; he looks so queer in your face, too, and makes his long fingers grasp and let go the coverlet like pinchers going by steam—he's a little 'un, that master of ours. Sometimes when he's up to his games, don't I wish I could take him by the collar, and hold his head over the walls of t'other world an hour; that would soon make him sing small, Zuc.'

"'But, Polly,' I asked, 'how did such a little fellow

get such a power over a lady like Miss Mary—one so brave, so pious? she's not afraid of the other world.'

"'That she aint; they have to look after her that she don't slip into it before she's sent for; poor dear, she doesn't like this here world at all; always saying hard things of it, and gives it odd names, such as, "a howling wilderness," "the land of the enemy," "the dustbin of creation." Then she takes another tack, clasps her long fingers in each other, and gives such a sweet look to the skies, and says, "Soon, O Lord, let this solitary place be made glad." "How long, Lord? wilt thou hide thyself for ever?" "Arise, O Sun of Righteousness; shake healing from thy wings upon the sores of sinners." "Dear Jesus! let thy blood be upon the nations of the earth, and let multitudes which no man can number find a home under thy wings." "Come, Lord Jesus, come quickly!" When she stops speaking this way, she looks down upon ye, and squeezes ye and clasps ye to her breast; she *is* a good 'un. She's like a good timepiece, Zucci; her works are all sound inside. She says the Spirit of the Lord set her works all right, and that the blood of Christ made them clean. Now, Murray's jest t'other way; his wheels are all wrong, and never been cleaned. He does need a righting and a washing, eh, Zucci?'

"'He does, Polly,' I replied, and asked how ever two persons so different became acquainted?

"She said, 'Zucci, Miss Mary was not always as she

is now. 'Tis not long since the Spirit brought the blood to her. When Murray went among the schools as a teacher, the boarding school Miss Mary attended was among them. She all at once took a fancy to master; she began it first; every time she had a chance she would say something, do something, or give him something; when she had a holiday she would spend a part of it with him; she followed him everywhere, jest like your shadow when ye're walking along the road on a summer day. She was very young then; her eyes were jest beginning to open, she had queer likings, took fancies to things and people that everybody else saw nothing in, and therefore she took a fancy to master. Catch any one with both eyes open make the same mistake. I know two, Zuc, that would never think of falling in love with master. All went on quietly for a while—not a soul smelt a rat. Murray and mother never dreamt of a blow-up. One holiday Miss Mary, instead of going home, spent the whole of it with the little man, and returned at the proper time in the evening to her school; somehow or other they were caught on the hop, the thing got wind, and the whole thing was blown to chips and sent sky-high. Miss Mary was taken from school, Murray was bundled neck-and-crop out of every school where he was engaged, and all the young ladies were taught, as one of their exercises, to call him the "Nasty, deep, and dangerous little man." So your master and mine had to hook it—he did so; remained in the dark and on the quiet for a while, and by degrees he sneaked behind the scenes, and became what he now is—a player and our master.'

"'But, Polly,' interrupting you, 'what became of Miss Mary?'

"'La! poor soul, she *did* suffer in the flesh. Her papa took a house in the country, removed from town, and fell to teaching her himself, and for months she was not allowed to step beyond the door unless he were with her. She used to walk about the lanes with her papa, and keep as close by his side as if she had been a lapdog led by a chain. At times the poor soul would be seen walking in the garden alone, her head bent forward, her eyes staring on the ground, and talking to herself; then she would stand still, look up and all round, wipe her eyes, walk on, go into the house, and not be seen again for hours. The poor dear was jest like a young 'un running down a hill, and before she can stop herself, lands right in the middle of a lot of furze, and when she's clearing 'em tears her clothes and scratches her legs, and, after having got shot of them, has to sit down and pin her frock and take the prickles out of her flesh, crying sore all the while, mind ye. This was jest what Miss Mary was doing the first year she was in the country. She had had her race, had landed among the furze, and had to finish it by pinning her frock and taking out the prickles. She, too, poor soul, was a-cryin all the while she was a-doin of it, mind ye; but she got shot of her prickles in a strange way. About a stone's-throw from where she lived an old gentleman had built a little chapel, in the corner of his property that lay nearest their garden-wall. Of a Sunday this old gentleman used to gather in the people of the village and preach to them. Mary used to lean over the wall and listen when they were singing their hymns. At last she resolved to slip out and get into a corner of the chapel and hear him preach. On the Sunday she went. Just as she came in the old man was reading out the text—"And yet there is room." The words went right smack through her heart, Zuc, and gave her such a turn. She cried, prayed, and trembled all over, and has never been the same as she was before—became a different woman altogether—regular changed. When she went home from chapel she rushed into the drawing-room and fell on her father's neck, and, bursting into tears, she cried, "Papa, O papa, will you forgive me for all the past? 'Yet there is room'—Jesus says it; yes, room even for your Mary in his heart; in his church here, in his heaven yonder. Yes, the blood has done it—made room in heaven even for Mary Drew, the scarlet sinner!' Yes, papa, through that precious blood, without one good action—nay, without one good thought on my part, your Mary may enter heaven NOW, and stand white as snow in the very presence of God! O precious Saviour! precious blood! But, 'tis true, the blessed Bible says it! Carry me to my room, that I may die and go up and enjoy it!"

After she had said all I've told ye, and a great deal more, which I forget now, for as often as I've heard it from Mother Murray and from Miss Mary's own lips. When she had said all this she fainted, and had to be carried up-stairs. Her papa, who, when she entered the room, had been reading, let the book fall out of his hand, became so frightened, that for a moment he could only stare, and sat as quiet as if he had been turned into stone; but when she fainted he sprung to his feet, and when the servants came into the room he was kneeling beside her, saying—"Mary! my poor Mary, I have forgiven you! I did forgive you! I will forgive my child—my only child!" While the old man was kneeling and sobbing these words into her ear, and the servants were bathing of her with cold water, she began to move; after a little while she sat up, and, putting her thin white hand on her father's cheek, she murmured, "Forgive me, forgive me!" then, as if something she had forgot had come suddenly into her mind, she quietly clasped her hands, and, looking through a smile on all around, whispered the name of Jesus, and was carried upstairs, whispering all the way, "Jesus! 'Yet there is room!' Oh! his precious blood!" She was unable to leave her room for months, and while she was lying a-bed she read nothing but the Bible, and prayed. The servants said, waken at any hour ye would hear prayer or verses of the Bible in Miss Mary's room. The old man who preached in the chapel was allowed to come and see her, and when she was able she was allowed to walk out with him along the lanes. What a sight it was to see the old man, with silver hair on his head and silver hair on his chin, leading Miss Mary about! she leaning on his arm as pale as moonlight, as thin as a ghost, with a plain cottage-bonnet on, a big shawl pinned round her throat, and a big Bible under her arm—the poor dear. The blood and the Spirit had done a good stroke of work in her heart, anyhow! When the old man spoke of her, he used to call her a new creature in Christ Jesus, and, like Miss Mary, he always said the blood and the Spirit did it. Even Mother Murray used to say, when Mary would be leaving the house after a visit, "Ah, how changed, not like the same woman she once was—quite a different creature!" but SHE never added, the blood and the Spirit did it. Yet she knew what did it; Miss Mary often told her; I've heard her say it again and again to her, that the blood of Christ and the Spirit of God could and did save the chief of sinners; free of expense, too; ay, and jest as they stood upright in their clothes, with all their sins about them; but, Zuc, she did not believe her, that's why she was mum about what did it. Even I, who have been in a reformatory and have no rich relations, half believe what did it; that was what they always said at the reformatory, too. The blood and the Spirit's work was all the talk there. Zuc, do you believe it? Do you know what

I sometimes think, that when the Spirit and the blood *do* meet in a feller's heart they must stun him like a thunder-clap, and do a something inside which makes them very different outside. I ask sometimes, when thinking about Miss Mary, if EVER they will meet in me, but something in me says—"No, Poll, you're too rum a gal;" and if there's a Bible near me when the shakes are on me I stare at it, pass on, and feel as if I was going by a cemetery at night. But, Zuc, I'd better bring my yarn to a close, in case the little man and his mother should come and put their foot through it. Well, Miss Mary grew stronger and stronger every day, and she was so different now that her papa allowed her to go where she liked and do what she liked. All the summer, while she lived in the country, she went from house to house, speaking to them about Jesus, the Spirit, and the blood. On Sundays she taught a class in the little chapel, and whenever there was any one ill you would see her at all hours, wet or dry, cold or hot, on the trot, carrying a basket or a bundle full of little comforts to them. She did the same when she came to town for the winter. And as sure as winter came and went she visited the Murrays, and, after spending a little while with the mother, she would spend a little while with the son, after the style you witnessed in the 'Cell,' and so she got the name of the 'Spectre.'' As Poll reached this part of her tale, the sound of approaching footsteps made her change the subject and burst into a 'rattler,' and sent me to my spangle-picking. Now, sir, I'm certain you do not regret my stepping a little aside from my own history to give you Polly's sketch of Miss Mary Drew. Well, sir, that lady was, and is now, one of my very best earthly friends."

CHAPTER IX.

THERE were a few simple reflections suggested to the mind of the writer at this stage of Zuccani's narrative, which might also, in some measure, suggest themselves to the mind of the reader. Before the narrative is resumed it may not be unprofitable for the writer to reproduce them, nor for the reader to examine them.

When Columbus was nearing the American coast in his first voyage, his observant eye detected in the masses of drift that passed his ship some indications of the character of the country to which he was approaching. He discoursed of these to his crew, and thereby cheered them not a little. By means of them he lightened the burdens of the present, trained every eye to discern sunny glimpses of the future, and each man to believe that soon he would cast anchor in some quiet harbour on the shore of another world. We also are voyagers; certainly not to a land unknown. In the chart of the great navigator America was not indicated—it had yet to be discovered; in our chart—the blessed Bible, the "shining shore" of the country to which we are steering stands out against the horizon in crisp and definite outline. To him who sails by this chart faithfully there can be no real danger; true some may have to outride the intervening sea on boards, and some on broken pieces of the ship, but every soul that sails according to the authorised chart shall be found on the shores of Canaan at the break of day—that day that knows no night. Not only shall there not be one voyager absent, but one hair of the head of any of them shall not be missing. Our chart is faultless, and our landing secured beyond all doubt. Notwithstanding the unerring character of the chart and the perfect assurance of reaching the shore, yet, through the weakness of the flesh, every voyager at times feels the toils and trials of the present to be severe, and beholds the future present itself to the eye in a light so questionable as to be at a loss to determine whether it shall be enjoyed amid the splendours of a fadeless day, or endured amid the horrors of an endless night. In such moments the soul, like a stricken deer, retires to the shade, wrapped up in its miserable self, and feels alone, destitute, afflicted, tormented. Often may such a wounded spirit be inspired with fresh energy, led to see some point formerly unseen set down in the chart, and catch glimpses of the land that is afar off, by narrowly and prayerfully examining those clumps of moral drift that float across life's solemn main. Such was the emblem under which the following reflections rose in my mind. In this part of Zuccani's narrative I thought there came into view some of that drift which, when examined in the light of the Word, gives much interest to the present of human life, and, when pierced and permeated by the light of the sure word of prophecy, affords some instructive glimpses of its future.

That there is another world beyond the grave the Word of God has put beyond and above all dispute. Human nature, crushed thing though it be; creation, blighted though it be; and providence, in its nature awfully magnificent, and in some of its aspects far removed beyond man's comprehension though it be, abound in proofs of the same fact. That all men are moving and fast disappearing into that world is equally true. Also, far exalted beyond all cavil, by the same Word, is the stern fact that immediately before entering that world of endless life there is a solemn bar of judgment, before which small and great must stand; and that there a faithful account of the past of human life is demanded of every individual as he appears. The presiding Judge is no deputy, remember; he is none other than Jesus Christ—God Almighty. But this august Court is not only grave and fearfully interesting on account of the dignity of its Judge, but likewise on account of the solemn and unalterable consequences that follow its decisions in the case of each as he stands for trial before it. Every individual as he leaves this Court is forthwith consigned to a path of existence, along which he must move during a dreary eternity ever deepening in gloom; or to a career of ever varying joys, throughout a glorious future ever brightening. This one great fact makes the life of man sublime! How does every thoughtful and believing man's excitement increase, intensify, and burn, when his eye falls on the plain and simple facts that are to guide the findings of the Judge! Simply thoughts, words, and deeds! Yes, reader, and these not only collected from the grand occasions of life, such as the hour of devotion, of suffering, or of daring, but as they bubble up on all occasions to the surface of every-day life, in kitchen and drawing room, workshop and counting-house, palace and cottage; yes, all, as they have risen throughout the individual life of man, as it wears away among the hours, places, and circumstances of his earthly lot. These three simple ingredients above all else, next to the decease accomplished at Jerusalem, most deeply tinge the everlasting life of the soul of man. How deeply personal is the whole matter, too; what could be more so, than in open Court to be confronted with one's own thoughts, words, and deeds, especially when it is remembered that, according to the rule of the Court, palliating, softening, glossing, and explaining away are excluded. Nor does this solemn moment in the life of man lose any of its importance when examined in the light of Scripture. Read for yourself the following statements: "For the Lord seeth not as man seeth; for man looketh on the outward appearance, but the Lord looketh on the heart."—1 Samuel xvi. 7. "But I say unto you, that every idle word that men shall speak, they shall give account thereof in the day of judgment. For by thy words thou shalt be justified, and by thy words thou shalt be condemned."—Matthew xii. 36, 37. "For we must all appear before the judgment seat of Christ; that every one may receive the things done in his body, according to that he hath done, whether it be good or bad."—2 Corinthians v. 10.

That a day so awfully important awaits every man we doubt not for a moment. Apart from all other evidences, we believe it on the *bare* Word of God. That its investigations will be so minute as to weigh, sift, and ascertain the drift of *every* thought of the heart, word of the lip, and deed of the life, we as fully believe on the simple authority of the Word of God. That every moment of the succeeding immortality of the soul will take an ever-deepening tinge, an ever-widening range from this day's proceedings, we as sincerely and as fully believe. But frequently has the question arisen in the mind of the writer, Can an hour, so momentous—a coming event, so pregnant with fate to man, come upon him so suddenly as to cast *no* shadow before it? The Word says its shadow darkens the door of every man so broadly, so clearly, as to leave him without excuse for any one sin of his whole life. The tracing of the projected shadow of this coming event, and the possible mode of its development, form the bulk of the reflections that rose in the mind of the writer as he listened to that part of Zuccani's narrative where the connection between Miss Drew and the Murrays is brought out. Man is so placed here that, should his life come to a close without his knowing and being reconciled to God, he is without excuse, because it is an undeniable feature of the Divine government, that wherever there is an intelligent creature, never, in any case, at any hour, nor in any place, is that creature without a witness for God before his eyes: "For the invisible things of him from the creation of the world are clearly seen, being understood by the things that are made, even his eternal power and Godhead; so that they are without excuse."

In every well-regulated kingdom there is not a province in which the power of the sovereign is not felt, or his person duly represented; for the right of the crown there are friends and witnesses, staunch and true, throughout the length and breadth of such a realm. If a rebel do but raise his head in any part of it he is immediately apprehended by judiciously-posted officers, and his guilt is brought home to him by a host of witnesses, of whose very existence he dreamt not till the moment he was put under arrest,

This is eminently a feature in the government of God. In no part of his vast dominions is his power unfelt; in no part of his empire is his person unrepresented. Among all the tribes of his intelligent creatures, there is not one around whose dwellings witnesses for Jehovah are not rife. How true is this, at least, of that part of his dominions we know best—the earth we inhabit. Over every roof-tree under which a son of Adam dwells there hovers a cloud of witnesses for God, a kind of domestic shekinah proclaiming God is near; yes, on every door-step throughout the living world there stands a messenger, a special messenger in the livery of heaven, with these words upon his lips, "Behold, I stand at the door and knock, a messenger for God." It matters not from what spot on earth a man wends his way to the grand Assizes, nor under what circumstances a man may have lived out his day; there is not one instance on record in which a man has ever been so placed, as at that tribunal to be able to say a single hour ever passed over his head in some part of which a monitory voice for God was not heard. It is the testimony of every conscience before God, that proofs of his eternal power and Godhead have burst upon it from every possible angle and corner; and with a testimony so simple and so clear, as to make all excuse for a life of sin impossible.

How vast in number, how varied in character are these unimpeachable witnesses for God! At one time it is some of the vast monuments of creation; the stars in their courses; the deep, with its noise of many waters; or some scene in which "the pastures are clothed with flocks; the valleys also are covered over with corn; they shout for joy." Again, it is some providence, with its miraculous arrangements as to time, place, and person. At another time it is a fellow-creature, with the love of Jesus in his heart, the law of love on his lips, and all the feelings of his nature in full cry after souls, that stands forth in a godly life, and proclaims, with a glowing tongue, there is a God who "so loved the world, that he gave his only begotten Son, that whosoever believeth in him should not perish, but have everlasting life." All men are surrounded with most of these witnesses, and many men go to the grave accompanied by all of them up to the last moment. Who can calculate the influence their testimony exerts in the adjustment of man's final doom?

But not to multiply instances, nor to enlarge the field of thought, let us approach this subject a little closer, and observe how it creeps out in the affairs of the Murray family.

Here is a man, not without ability; his mother descended from an educated and respectable ancestry. The young man has a good start in life; he is admitted as a teacher of his art into some of the largest and most respectable private educational institutions of the metropolis. In an evil hour he listens to the voice of the tempter; an evil thought is suggested, is cherished, and allowed to pass into a passion—a ruling passion. His freedom now is gone. Whither that passion leads he must follow; what it makes him he must be; and what it commands he must perform. In the course of events a boarding-school miss, emerging from her teens, crosses his path and is smitten with an affection for him—an affection at once romantic and pure. "A victim! a victim!" he whispers in his heart, and starts in pursuit! Yes, reader, that pale-faced maiden, with much of beauty, enriched and heightened by devotedness of purpose, eccentricity of character, and genuine warmth of heart, is to be the first victim. Every consideration of manliness; every motive prompting to honourable affection or mercy; every possible consequence to his victim and her aged father; every possible result in his own or his mother's case, are overpowered and caused to fade into dimness before the wild fire of his own feelings. The snare is laid. All the 'soft goods' (to use one of his own expressions, and meaning, by his own admission, all remonstrances from conscience within and warnings from God without) are thrown away; cunningly, silently, and covertly he works under ground. No unwary miss ever played so long with danger and so easily escaped. By his own confession, in the hearing of Polly, often has Mary's confidence in him as a man, and her innocence before him as a woman, made him pause, as does the helpless look of the lamb sometimes arrest for the moment the arm raised to slay it. In such moments he has been heard to confess, also, that he felt "as if the eye of God was looking him full in the face." Maidenly confidence and womanly innocence bore noble testimony, as God's witnesses, even to this unprincipled villain, and for the time they made his purpose falter and his foot tremble to advance. Occasionally Mary, too, would get glimpses of his designing nature; then would the little miscreant be compelled to retire abashed before the fire of her eye and the hard blows of her sturdy mind, and she in her turn be made to remember, fear, and think of the same God. As yet she was unable fully to read her man, and so for a season she lingered near because she loved him; and he, under the fatal impulse of his depravity, followed afar off, vainly dreaming of success, little comprehending the innocence and mettle of the melancholy miss just finishing her school days and her sampler, before escaping into womanhood, and seriously commencing life as her old father's housekeeper. And what Christian can contemplate this conflict of conscience in both cases, and the striking testimony for a present God maintained by the accusing thoughts of each, without being struck at the singular arrangements God hath made for leaving man without excuse for one sinful act in any part of his life? Had he triumphed and she fallen, both were equally without excuse. Yes, reader, in the act of sinning—although no stray passage from the Word, no apparently adverse providence from God, nor any warning from a human lip reach thee—if so much as one remonstrant cry be heard within the sinning soul, that cry is God's witness against thee, and thou art without the shadow of an excuse. How awful, then, must his condition be who turns his back upon a warning Bible, a frowning providence, a beseeching voice, and an accusing conscience! At last, as the sapper is sometimes anticipated and countermined, and his subterranean path laid open to the light of heaven by a counter-blast, so were the covered ways of the cunning dancer.

The whole affair is exposed, and the bird escapes the snare of the fowler. The matter reaches the ear of the father, and Mary is removed to the country. The destroyer is hunted from respectable society to herd with kindred spirits among back alleys, penny gaffs, and behind the scenes of second-rate theatres; the mother, too, who once had seen better days—purer days—on account of her easy virtue, is allowed to drift in the same direction. Now both have reached the very back settlements of modern civilisation; this guilty son and his more guilty mother have thrown away all their 'soft goods,' but still an open vision stares them in the face; even here the guilty pair are constantly reminded of the ceaseless presence of a holy God, sore against their will. Every day the joys of heaven and the woes of hell are warbled in their ears by the 'heavenlies' of Polly; yes, and more than confirmed by the wierd-like visits of that female Elijah—Mary Drew. Her sense of duty to Jesus, her pity for the soul of him who did much to ruin her's, carry her thither to preach Christ to him and his mother as their only way of escape. She does it faithfully, lovingly, and without dissimulation. Had the reader passed that forlorn house at the dead of night, when the revels ran high; its mistress gathered up like a heap of rags, blinking and dreaming in a corner under the influence of 'skyey'; the little dark-haired master smoking, and swearing, and speaking of himself great swelling words; pale-faced Zuccani looking into the fire and bitterly thinking of to-morrow; and Polly making the rafters ring with an Irish 'rattler' as she washed her supper-dishes—I say, had the reader seen and heard all this, could he have believed that not a day passed over that house but some testimony for God was raised, and not unfrequently the way of salvation preached plainly to its inmates by one of the most remarkable, most beautiful, and most polished of England's daughters? You could not come to such a conclusion from the scene before your eyes! Nevertheless, it was true. They were warned of God by his Word; they heard of his Son daily in hymns, and psalms, and spiritual songs, and in the beseeching voice of Mary. But the Murrays are not singular in this respect. Every slum and purlieu in the Christian world has its witnesses for God; there is not one in which he has left himself without a witness. And here we might notice in passing that the visitor, missionary, or minister who has to stand up in these dark places for a living Saviour, will do well not to ignore the kind of monitors with which God has followed them hitherto, but will show his wisdom in ascertaining what these were; and, with his gospel message following in their wake, he will find much goods laid up in store, simply waiting his arrival with the key and seal of the blessed Master to make them his, and on which very soon may be written, "Bought with blood;" "Holiness to the Lord."

That a reckoning so terribly strict and painfully minute as Scripture declares will take place at the bar of Christ, in the case of one so feeble and forgetful as man, is abundantly proved from the following fact. That for the purposes of justice, for the interpreting of his ways with man to his other intelligent creatures, and principally in furtherance of his ulterior purposes with man himself, God has so placed him among the laws of nature, and so related him to the other portions of creation, that, while he is working out his day here, he is also with his own hand writing his memoirs in fadeless characters in another place. The following illustration will make the matter simpler and clearer, perhaps.

It is recorded of the railway tubular bridge across the Menai Strait, that while serving the purposes of traffic it writes its own history. It is so constructed, and so laid on its supports, that by means of a delicate apparatus it denotes, on a prepared surface, the amount of expansion in its material from solar heat; the degree of pressure and motion imparted to it by the winds that beat upon it; also any alterations in its condition from the passing shower, and the amount of vibration in its whole bulk, arising from the various trains that roll through it. Thus, in the act of answering the object for which it was built, it also writes its own biography: these jottings may be translated into the language of men and written in a book. Man is so placed among the laws of nature, and among the elements of matter, that, while in the act of accomplishing his day below, he is also, by means of an apparatus remarkably delicate, on surfaces prepared and lasting, writing his own memoirs. The discoveries of modern science have proved, to a demonstration, that every atom of matter retains the impressions imparted to it. No motion ever impressed upon the atoms of matter, by natural causes or by human agency, is ever obliterated! The air, the earth, and the ocean, by this means, become "the eternal witnesses of the acts we have done." On this principle the air becomes one vast scroll, on which are written in characters that shall never die every utterance and whisper of the lips, whether they escape them as vows, prayers or promises, jeers or jests. Who does not feel, in presence of this fact, intuitively rising within him that prayer—"O Lord, keep of my lips the door." But here the wonder ceases not, for in virtue of the same law there is not a movement of the human frame but describes itself in lines that never grow dim on some enduring surface. Nay, more; not a particle leaves the human body, or is disengaged by its agency from that of any other, but starts forthwith on a path of influence that has no close, and retains the precise impulse received for evermore. Man's thoughts, words, and deeds, by this wonderful arrangement on the part of God, the moment they pass from him become immortal! With the pen of a ready writer, and with the accuracy and the activity of a recording angel, each writes the vicissitudes and sins of human life before God and in distant regions against the great day. Reader, think of meeting this second edition of thyself—unrevised, unregenerated, and uncorrected in that awful hour, when God shall reveal the secrets of all hearts by Jesus Christ! Do not these words—"The blood of Jesus Christ his Son cleanseth us from all sin," steal like music through thy soul in the prospect of such a spectacle? If not, you are yet in your sins.

When you contemplate in the light of this solemn truth the proceedings before the judgment seat of Christ, notwithstanding their all-comprehensive minuteness, do you see any practical difficulty to their taking place in the case even of a creature so frail, so vile, and so forgetful as man? Do you see any difficulty to their taking place in your own case? I trow not. Nay, does not this fact proclaim in your ear that when the books are opened the inquiry will be searching, even to the dividing asunder of the joints and marrow?

Reader, are you a young man? Between these two lines of witnesses you are threading your way along life's high road to the grave, to the bar of God, and to eternity. Life is a solemn thing, "and the grave is not its goal." On every side a host of friends, of facts, testify to your conscience of the Lord that made you, of the Lord that died for you, and that will judge you. Do you respond, "I care for none of these things," and "I make no profession?" That is not the point. Have you been warned of his existence; have you ever been convinced of your lost condition, and often been informed of the way of escape? You know you have, and your conscience partly confesses the fact; this makes you responsible to God, and without excuse at his bar. Are you converted, and so seen your condition before God, as to be glad to fly to the fountain for cleansing? Under the solemn circumstances of a judgment close at hand this is your reasonable service. But if you are not, and, because you have neither said yea nor nay to the offers of Christ, are now fondly dreaming you may wash your hands clean of the matter, reader, in the sight of God this is the most ungracious mode of rejecting the Son possible to the creature.

Young man, bethink thyself. Although thou hast

not chosen Christ, and hast whispered in thy secret soul, "I will not have him to reign over me," thou art not free of him. Thou must stand before the judgment seat of that same Jesus, and there confront, recorded by thine own hand, every thought that ever passed through thine own heart; every utterance and whisper that ever escaped thy lips; and behold, inscribed with an unerring pencil, a faultless outline of every movement of thy frame. Reader, dost thou think that out of Christ thou couldest venture to behold such a spectacle? behold *thyself* dissected and exposed in thy thoughts, words, and deeds before an assembled universe, and in the cloudless light of the day of judgment? Thou knowest in thy conscience thou couldest not; thou wouldest rather die a thousand deaths than pass through such an ordeal! Yet, reader, thou feelest and knowest in thine inmost soul that such an ordeal is before thee—that such a day awaits thee. Linger not one moment longer on debatable ground. Heed the warnings ten thousand friendly witnesses for God afford thee. Receive the report of the gospel concerning Jesus, and accept heaven's artless, unencumbered plan of escape—believe and live. Beneath the shadow of his wing, bathed and baptized in his blood, and wrapped in his spotless righteousness, thou hast nothing to fear from the handwriting on the wall. In thy case, and on thy behalf, it is scanned by the eye of God through the rent vail of a Redeemer's flesh, and thou art free.

My reader, are you a young woman? here there are grave matters for your gentle thoughts. You, also, must appear before the judgment seat of Christ. Your every thought, word, and deed are also gone before you. Blush not; even your secret soul will be revealed and made to glisten in the light of Christ's eye in that terrible day of the Lord. Do you doubt it? Think you not you also move about in the same cloud of witnesses? Read for yourself the following message once sent by the living God to the young women of Zion: "Moreover the Lord saith, Because the daughters of Zion are haughty, and walk with stretched forth necks and wanton eyes, walking and mincing as they go, and making a tinkling with their feet: therefore the Lord will smite with a scab the crown of the head of the daughters of Zion, and the Lord will discover their secret parts. In that day the Lord will take away the bravery of their tinkling ornaments about their feet, and their cauls, and their round tires like the moon, the chains, and the bracelets, and the mufflers, the bonnets, and the ornaments of the legs, and the head-bands, and the tablets, and the ear-rings, the rings, and nose-jewels, the changeable suits of apparel, and the mantles, and the wimples, and the crisping-pins, the glasses, and the fine linen, and the hoods, and the veils. And it shall come to pass, that instead of sweet smell, there shall be stink; and instead of a girdle, a rent; and instead of well set *hair*, baldness; and instead of a stomacher, a girding of sackcloth; and burning instead of beauty."—Isaiah iii. 16—24. Could you have believed that this was a stray leaf from the book of God's remembrance? It is even so. How fearfully strict is each entry, and how terribly minute! the haughty walk, the stretched neck, the very movements of the feet, and the glances of the eye; the number of head-dresses, mantles, and gowns, and all the jewels distinctly named. This is very particular work—very. Yet it is the way, the only way, they keep accounts in heaven: and all about trifling things, too—the gewgaws of a young woman's toilet and wardrobe, for nothing is said here about thoughts, words, and deeds. Dream not these are left out, for if the Lord be so minute in things so trivial as dress, will he be less so, think you, in the weightier matters of the soul? Impossible! What a powerful argument, if unconverted, should this be for you to fly to a Saviour. Give him no rest neither day nor night till he present you to God washed in his blood and adorned with his righteousness, and beautified within by his Spirit as a bride adorned for her husband. And to your dying day remember the cloud of witnesses that hover round your steps amid the secrets of your toilet; in the open sunlight of the highway or under the cloud of night; amid the gaieties of the domestic party or the solemnities of the house of prayer. And, now, what is really your condition before God? He knows all. Without a shiver in your conscience, as you at this moment stand, could you meet him with his open book? No, sister; out of Christ God is a consuming fire. Oh! then, hasten while the day of grace lasts to an entreating Saviour. At any moment you may be at his bar. To the blood! to the blood! sister.

But, reader, art thou an aged sinner? in this matter of the witnesses there is much to rouse thee. In thy case there is not a moment to be lost. Thy record is on high, and, like the prophet's roll, it is written without and within—a few more jottings, and it will be finished. Old man, thy life's story will soon be like some lettered monument standing in the open field; with the sunlight falling all around it, every passer-by may read it, and know thee from thy cradle to thy grave! What an exposure is this for a life of unforgiven sin, apart from its consequences! Come, man, creep ye also to the fountain—the day is far spent, to be sure, but stretch forth thine hands, his are able to pull thy weary soul into life from under the very ribs of death!

And, now, dear Christian reader, there is nothing in all this to alarm thee. There is much in it to make thee careful, watchful, diligent, and prayerful, but also much to cheer thee; thy silent tears, thy sleepless nights, on account of sin and souls, are all registered, and undying evidence will they give before God, angels, men, and devils—proving to all whose thou art and whom thou servest.

Trusting this digression will be forgiven, let us now return with renewed zest to the troubled story of poor *Zuccani*.

CHAPTER X.

"By degrees I was fully instructed in all the mysteries of stage-dancing, and by degrees, slow and sure, Murray gave me the full benefit of the iron breeches, which, after sundry applications and much pain, imparted an astonishing suppleness to my limbs. In a short time I was earning bread and praise for myself, and money for master.

"I will not tax your patience, nor insult your feelings, by telling you *all* I have witnessed behind the scenes or in the 'green-room.' But, sir, allow me to give you *some idea* of what I've passed through in this respect; it will give completeness to my simple story, and give you some idea of what Christ has had to do for me till I was able, as I now am, to stand before you, living in body and believing in soul.

"The great day—the very greatest day of my existence had come; so I was informed one morning at breakfast. I was to appear before a London audience, and prove to the Murrays for what God had made me—they being the sole judges. Such was the substance of the conversation at the breakfast-table on the morning of that day in the evening of which I was to appear in the play of 'The Lost Child.'

"For days before I had been nearly danced and fiddle-bowed to death. Every possible attitude into which the human body can be put, short of being taken to pieces and the life poured out, I had been in. During the same period I had been flattered, frightened, and cursed in all the syllables of play poetry; and, finally, Mrs. Murray prepared me for the evening's work in the morning by the following speech: that if I failed 'the gas would be sucked out of the brackets, the fire put out on the hearth;' nay, my failure would take the bread out of their mouths, and scatter them paupers over the face of the earth.

"The part assigned to me in the evening performance was one of dumb show—simply dancing. Only one speech fell to my lot, and it was one line in length; but the preparations as to the style and mode of delivery were weeks long, and accompanied by many a shirt-full of sore bones. At length the hour arrived, and Murray, mother, and I started in a cab for the scene of trial, and we were put down at a large house which we entered by a small wicket, bearing the inscription, 'Stage Door.' Trembling, and almost delirious with excitement, I descended with them to the 'green-room.' Before us were two sets of small doors, painted green and white, ranging three on each side of a larger door leading to the stage. One set of doors admitted the ladies to their dressing apartments, and the others the gentlemen to theirs. Each apartment was square and well supplied with everything necessary for the toilet. In front of these doors was an open space under the stage, and over it were dispersed, in groups, the actors, actresses, and ballet-girls of the establishment. Oh, what a scene! garish and exciting to the eyes of a poor soul who now witnessed it on a large scale for the first time. Men and women, arrayed in all sorts of costume, were distributed in knots over the open space; a merry song rising and floating over the heads of one group, betting and wagering in a second cluster, and a third group weltering, tugging, and pulling at each other in a game of 'halfpenny scramble;' in a fourth they were measuring stature and limbs—they that excelled in such were paying or being paid, and the money thus collected was to be 'melted' in strong drink the first opportunity. Here and there stray individuals might be met, like ghosts, sitting in corners, filled with anger or strong drink, or something which rendered them of a different communion from all that were moving around them; another, all alone, too, was pacing backwards and forwards, reciting his part and striking at his shadow with his cane for lack of other foe; and yet another, deep in shade and all alone, also deep in conflict with something more substantial than his shadow—the sorrows of his heart, caused by some muddled love-story, or more likely with the sweet remembrance of a narrow escape from some adroit creditor, who very nearly saved our friend the trouble of appearing on the boards for the evening. A variety was occasionally lent to the scene by a quarrel between two girls, or a tongue-to-tongue battle between the enraged manager and a rebel actor, or the vulture-like movements of a sprinkling of fast young men, swaggering, swearing, and courting, freely distributing money they had never earned. Add to the whole, Mother Murray gliding in every direction, the familiar of all, the beloved of none, her eyes lost in smiles, her foot and hand speaking louder than many tongues, and her breath indicating the presence of 'skyey' influences. One other element, and the picture is complete. Far aloft, as of a sea in trouble, might be heard the noise of that dreadful creature—the 'public.' It was waiting to be amused and gulled, but with very bad grace and no patience.

"I was now arrayed in black velvet and spangles, to represent the 'long lost child.' This I could have done without velvet or tinsel—I was lost in reality. All around me yawned one vast gulf of corruption, and in any direction I looked could discover no friendly hand stretched out to help. At last a bell was rung, and the whole mass moved up-stairs to the stage, each finding a place among the scenery. The friends, fast and slow, settled down on chairs, or what accommodation they could find. Bell the second rings, up rises the curtain, and Murray and I appear before a mansion on the edge of a wood, amid the applause of the gallery. I was dressed like a simple youth on a holiday from school; he was habited like a villain. The scene opened by an attempt on his part to allure me from home. For a moment the sea of human faces and the noise stunned me. Murray was prepared for this; a murmured oath and the promise of the fiddle-bow removed the feeling. Out of sight of the audience, full in view of all the stage, stood Mrs. Murray, with her clenched fist, her eye full on me, the very picture of wrath—no, sir, anger turned into a woman. I was at last put in motion by the music, and performed my part with applause. On retiring behind the scenes all praised me, Mother Murray excepted. I now felt at ease for the rest of the night.

"But, sir, what a farce is the stage as a teacher of morals! A grand mistake! Here is my first night's experience behind the scenes on a grand scale. The part played by one man—that of a monkey—struck me much; disguised as one of these animals, he leaped and frisked about among the painted trees of the painted wood, to the intense delight of the whole audience; it laughed as if it had been one immense face; his part was done to perfection. But follow this man-monkey off the stage, where there is NO paint, and where everything IS what it seems. There he is leaning his head against a post, smiting his breast—almost weeping. His grief is caused by thoughts of his home, for it is desolate; his wife, for she is bad; and of his own way of life, for it is corrupt—one immense evil deed. These things, when they met in his memory, often unmanned him, I was told, as they were doing that night. But his part comes round again, and he must gambol—almost fly—before the common eye; his crust depends upon it. Oh, what a sham is that man tumbling about there! Behind the curtain, a statue of lead from remorse and sorrow; before the same curtain, against his will, for a bit of bread, he becomes a trifle light as air: for a heart as light as a monkey's he would give all the world. In that play everything was real but its truthfulness. Its trees and fruits were shams, for they were painted; every man and woman in it was a lie—a human lie; they were *everything* but what they seemed. The bereaved parents in this same piece, an actor and his wife, had to be separated by the manager, and prevented blackening one another's eyes immediately before they appeared; that's their life among the pullies. Let us follow them to the boards. There they are, bemoaning their loss among the painted trees of a desolate island, professing the deepest attachment for each other; she embracing him with an arm yet aching from the blows of his hand. That very hand, held aloft to the painted heavens, its owner meanwhile vowing it never had been, and never would be, employed but in the holy offices of protecting and administering to her comfort, a few minutes before was stained with her blood! In the same scene, and at the same moment, Murray and I were in a huge box under a mock tree; under its lid he was blowing me up, almost strangling me, for some little blunder I had made. Above the lid of this same box sat the man-monkey, a martyr to heart-pain; and the piece closes by the whole party, monkey and all, moving off in a boat, singing praise for the recovery of the 'lost child' in hymns they did not feel, to a God they did not know.

"Shortly before it pleased God to remove me from the wretched home of Murray, and the still more wretched profession of a dancing-boy, I was called upon to witness the first appearance of death in the actor's dwelling. That event formed a tragedy in which every performer appeared in REAL character. In this piece everything was real but the grief.

"A Mrs. West, among others, frequented Murray's house during the season. Under another name, for three years previous to my becoming an inmate of Murray's house, she had delighted the playgoers of all the second-rate houses as a tragedian of the very highest order. Her abilities were such as to have carried her triumphantly to the first place in any of the great houses of the metropolis—such was the general opinion of her powers off the stage as well as on it. Strong drink made her advancement impossible.

"She was a tall dark woman, of very commanding figure, remarkable for the length of her arms and the tones of her voice; if human talk could have been set to music, her's might. She had a remarkably solemn countenance, and when she spoke a feeling of awe stole over the hearer's person; sometimes in fits of intemperance she would recite portions of plays till the flesh seemed to creep on the spectator's bones.

One night, I well remember witnessing a real display of her power. Over their cups words ran high between Mrs. Murray and her; such a scene would have adorned any stage, and entranced any audience; without design it was the very perfection of acting. Her arms were flying about like the sails of a windmill; her eyes glared on her opponent through a green kind of fire, just as when those of a wild beast are seen in the dusk of the evening; her voice descended from a shriek to a deep bass; and her foot kept time with the tread of a horse. After her own fashion my little missis was quite a match for her. The one, a mixture of nature and the very highest art; the other, nature, from which all art was expelled when in a blaze. The words of the actress came forth like polished shafts, the pointed steel of which was taken chiefly from old plays. Those of missis fell among the feelings of the actress like bits of fire among gunpowder—always producing an explosion. One flight of missis' burning words brought the actress to red heat, and she in return poured on the little woman's head the whole gall of her soul through one of Queen Margaret's speeches in 'Richard the III.' Standing her full height, she uttered in fierce tones these dreadful words—

'"Stay, dog! for thou SHALT hear me.
If heaven have any grievous plague in store
Exceeding those I can wish upon thee,
Oh, let them keep it, till thy sins be ripe,

And then hurl down their indignation
On thee, the troubler of my poor soul's peace!
Thy friends suspect for traitors whilst thou livest,
And take deep traitors for thy friends!
No sleep close up that deadly eye of thine!"'

"Mrs. Murray stopped this burst of human wrath, every word of which seemed to pierce her heart through and through, by falling on her knees. Whilst in this attitude she raised her hands over her head, and shrieked—

"'Thy vile tongue can do me no harm! Look, viper! before heaven I can smite my breast and say, Soul, be of good cheer, I have overcome the world; I care not—fear not! although a pile of serpents like you, whose top touched the sky, hissed fire in my face and weltered round me, their slime would not cling to me! I'm not of your kidney! Go it! the candle's dying! in another moment it will have its last flash!'

"As these last words fell from her lips Murray came in. He stared; astonishment fell over him; like a cloak, it covered the little man from head to foot—a feather would have knocked him down. I retreated into the street; its cool air was a mercy to me. I was so frightened that I asked myself was I among devils? God only knows the deep impression that scene made on my mind. It was a sermon, sir, preached by devils! I wandered about till it was time to go to bed. On returning to the house all was comparatively quiet, and a few more friends dropped in during my absence. They were standing round the actress; she had gone off in a fit of laughing hysterics. Such a picture! her hair flowing round her face and shoulders, and the noise of her laughter resembling that made by a bird-starver's rattle; her body was all in motion and her face wet with tears. I got bewildered and scared, and crept to my bed in the dark, where I lay sleepless and feverish till the noise below died away—long after midnight. In the morning all was quiet, as is the sea-shore on a morning succeeding a storm, where nothing is left to tell of its uproar save a few floating spars. Let the above sketch suffice as an exhibition of Mrs. West living: let us now behold her dying.

"How dreadful was the game played by these two desperate women. The actress lived apart from her husband on a weekly allowance, with extras in case of ill health. Often have they extorted money from Mr. West under the head of 'sick extras;' Mrs. Murray always played the part of liar and extortioner. Often has the poor husband between the pieces hurried to the den to see an afflicted wife, and found only a drunken one, his affection rewarded by foul abuse. The last act of the tragedy was drawing nigh; the dying scene was at hand; Death was at the door. When they looked not for him he silently stole across the stage, and laid his hand on the abandoned Mrs. West. The following morning she was in eternity, all her sins clinging to her soul!

"That night in which I first appeared in a large house, to please Murray she consented to appear. Some days before she had been drinking hard, and from cold and exposure her health was completely shattered. From excitement and drink she was seized with cholera and carried off the stage, and taken in a cab to Murray's house. The first—almost the only words she uttered were—

"'It's no joke this time—this is death. Oh, my poor soul!'

"The whole house was deeply moved. The doctor, who had followed her from the theatre, pronounced it a case of the very worst form of cholera; he pronounced it fatal. Mrs. Murray hurried off to West—this time not the messenger of his wife, but the messenger of Death, for just as she was leaving the house the wretched actress had died in the greatest agony and the deepest remorse. In a few minutes Mrs. Murray returned with the husband. In an agony of despair and affection the broken-hearted comedian embraced all that was mortal of his wife. Poor fellow! the night before he had held hundreds in a ceaseless roar of laughter: had the curtain risen on him that morning, his condition would have made as many weep.

"But, sir, how terrible is death in a house where Christ is unknown! how much more terrible must it be in the soul of a dying sinner, to which Christ is a stranger—such an one does die hard; but, oh, sir, who can *think* of the reception of a Christless soul on its emerging from the Valley of Death into the immediate presence of God, unwashed, unsanctified, and unredeemed!

"There stood Mrs. Murray at the feet of her she had helped to ruin, fearful thoughts rushing through her soul the while. She seemed intensely anxious to know if Death had left the dwelling, and if all his work were done. Well she knew her *own* accounts for eternity were messed and muddled, and in her case, at any rate, her looks seemed to say, ruin—eternal ruin would have been the result had her name been included in the summons that called Mrs. West to the Grand Assizes on high. The little dancing-master sat in silence on the end of a table biting his nails, musing deeply. Polly was eyeing master: the first opportunity she whispered into my ear, in a manner becoming the occasion—

"'Zuc, you see how quiet master is now; he's obliged to look over the walls of t'other world. Do you know what he is anxious to know, if any of us could tell him?—when Death, with Mrs. West in his arms, will quit the house, and if he is likely to have anyone else to keep 'em company.'

"Polly herself seemed much awed, but spoke little: if she was heard at all, it was humming, in a subdued tone, some of her sweetest 'heavenlies.' After all was over—the actress stretched upon her bier, and every yard of anything white so disposed of as to hide every yard of anything not white in the dreary dwelling, a number of professionals began to arrive. Every second-rate house in London seemed to send a representative to that death-bed. Such an assembly of mourners! Tragedians, comedians, dancers, and clowns! all wearing a face put on for the occasion. What a spectacle! The silence was only broken at intervals by a whispered extract from the death-scene of some play: if a joke did arise it was hideous, for it wore grave-clothes. The Bible, where was *it?* Neither in the pockets, on the lips, nor in the hearts of any mourner in that house. The act of God that wound that fallen woman in her shroud entered not among their thoughts. The blessed Jesus and his redemption were shadows as unreal as any shadows in their own Christmas fairy-land. By the time I retired to rest I left some snoring, others winking from strong drink, simply silent because they could not help it: those with whom the blessing of speech remained were rehearsing the follies and larks of her who not long before that midnight hour had rehearsed them in another place and to a different audience.

"This event made me heartily sick of an actor's life: three years of it had come and gone. This death-bed led to the emancipation of myself, body and soul—it brought my father on the scene.

CHAPTER XI.

"ONE cold, clear, moonlight night, as I sat by the fire brooding over the past, especially the death-bed scene and the conduct of all parties it brought to the house, I was disturbed by a smart rapping at the door. On its being opened, how amazed was I to behold my father! yet it *was* he—dressed like a gentleman, too. In a moment he embraced me, kissed me, and called me his boy. In a moment all parties in the dwelling, from different apartments, were standing round us. Questions in scores were put to him as to his health, concerning mother, his worldly prospects, but especially the object of his evening visit. After some replies had been made, and Poll had returned with a whole bottle of 'skyey,' Murray and mother, with my father, retired to another room, leaving me, as usual, alone with Polly, busy at work. I drew nearer the fire, and, resting my head upon my hands, looked into it and felt as if I were reading a book, its curling smoke, dancing flames, and red-hot coals forming the pictures on its pages. Whilst I was reading my flaming story, and staring at the burning faces that were grinning at me among the live coals, I was startled by a burst of loud words, followed by the heavy thump as of a clenched fist on the table. The words that fell first upon my ear were from the lips of Murray.

"'Now, Footy, "To be, or not to be? that is the question."'

"A driving of chairs drowned the reply. The next moment they were in the room beside me, my father's eye glancing with fire, and shouting, at the top of his voice—

"'Be! it shall be now—even this very moment. Zuc, pack up your traps, and prepare for leaving this hornets' nest!'

"In less time than it took to utter the command I was down-stairs, my whole wardrobe dangling in a spotted handkerchief. Amid a shower of evil words and imprecations from both sides I left that wretched home, without a sob or a sigh. One regret only dwelt in my heart: I sorrowed deeply to leave poor Polly. There she stood amid the Babel of curses and accusations, silent and thoughtful, a statue of flesh. As I shook her by the hand, I could not help exclaiming—

"'May God bless you, dear soul! for your kindness, constancy, and sympathy to me; and in your evil hour may some father come, and whisper in your ear, "Polly, this very moment leave this nest of hornets!" God speed the time!'

"She answered me with tears and by pointing to the crown of her head, which was her way of saying, 'Never show the white feather!'

"It was now far in the night. The streets were quiet, cold, and clean; a sharp wind was whistling along the alleys, and the moon rode high in the heavens, diffusing a light so clear that the chimney shadows lay on the grey pavement as if painted with tar. On leaving Murray's we wended our way down one alley after another. For the greater part of our walk father spoke not one word to me; he kept a little ahead of me, his hair and coat-skirts floating on the wind, and his hat lying back off his forehead. In this manner we continued our march—I behind, he in advance, continuously muttering to himself, and brandishing his cane over his head, as if to parry the blow of a foe,—to me invisible. We at last emerged into a wide street, which we crossed, and after threading our way through a lane, which led us out near Hungerford Bridge, we continued our journey over it. When about the middle of the bridge he paused; turning to me, and, laying his hands heavily on my shoulders, he said, in great excitement,

"'Zuc, do you love me—now, at this moment? Have I been cruel to you? Confess this moment all you feel towards me as your father. Out with it, I say, *now*. Make a clean breast of all; otherwise, let the river hide us both from the coming morning.'

"I instinctively fell on my knees and confessed my affection.

"'Enough, enough,' he cried; 'I'm satisfied, child. I still have one that does love me a little.'

"The approach of two gentlemen caused us to move on. He became gradually calmer, adjusted his hat, and began to talk a little kindly to me. A burden had fallen from his weary soul. The Murrays had made him believe that I did not love him, and that to them I

"LET THE RIVER HIDE US BOTH FROM THE COMING MORNING"

life of me I could not believe that my present circumstances were real. How unlike was Mary Sandeman, the lady at whose table I now sat, to the she-wolf I had just been torn from. Here we were in a kitchen whose furniture was shining as if newly polished, and its floor as white from scrubbing as if newly planed. Here and there against the walls hung pink cards with Scripture texts on them, and on its shelves, peeping from between shining tins and polished candlesticks, were Bibles, books, and tracts. Not one mask, foil, or fiddle in the dwelling. And when I turned to old Mary, as she sat in her elbow-chair, full of grace and truth, I did think it must be a dream. But, sir, it was not a dream; Mary Sandeman was real, her kitchen was real, and her sweet home was to me one of the grandest realities I had yet met with in my life.

"Miss Sandeman was a lady about sixty years of age, in stature about the middle size, rather slim in build, hair nearly grey and falling in ringlets over her temples; her countenance was rather square, her cheeks tinged with a fine soft peach-red, which set off the mildest brown eyes I ever saw. When she spoke, these eyes seemed to soften into masses of heaven's own dew; but if Jesus were the theme they would brim up till they ran over, her chest would move with her utterance, and her words fall on the ear warm with the glow of her heart, the dwelling-place of her religion. All the time I lived with her I never once heard her speak without seeing a smile on her face.

She was real in what she did, real in what she said, and God alone knows how real she was in her love to himself. It was 'Glory to God in the highest' with Mary in everything, to the taking of a drink of water up to the holiest act of the Christian life; yet so meekly did she move about in her daily life, and so really did she love Christ, that all *felt* and all esteemed the gospel in Mary's presence. She was remarkably well versed in Scripture, and the commonest conversation *she* could make interesting, and always beautiful, from a singular skill in the art of fitting texts into it. Her talk resembled those pavements of various coloured stones, which present to the eye a face or a flower. She so used the words of God in her talk as to make them present to the heart's eye the Cross of Calvary, the merciful Jesus, or the shining way up to heaven's gate. She lived partly by her needle and partly on a small annuity settled upon her by her only brother, a wine merchant in the city. She was, in her leisure moments, a physician to souls in trouble. She took a deep interest in the welfare of every one within her reach; the more so if they had a crook in their lot. How I used to sit and hear her tell of the struggles of spirit among her friends, and most of all the plan she adopted to get father to consent to allow me to stay with her. How the dear saint would laugh when she came to that part of the agreement wherein he handed over to her my stomach, reserving to himself the right of education and making a man of me.

"She gave me a hint the first day I spent with her as to father's intentions with me. How I stared when she told me that in a day or two I was to be entered a day pupil in a Roman Catholic school, where I was to be educated for a season; and, if my conduct justified it, I would be apprenticed to some respectable trade, through the influence of the school trustees! All the horrors of my former days came crowding into my mind. A big cross lay on my lot. I seemed once more to move in the thickest darkness. But, sir, I had this time a friend who dealt in nothing but 'heavenlies'—a Polly, too; how strange! But Jesus knew my hour was near. The good time was coming; the happy day was dawning. Miss Sandeman often lifted up my head by her tender sayings. Patting me on the shoulder and peering into my eyes she would say—

"'Fear not, Zucci; I see the bow in the cloud you so much dread. All God's clouds have silver linings; wait till his mercy opens them up.'

"In my home, happiness dwelt; in my heart, sadness. I dreaded that school as I did Murray's unpacking-room. Was I again to be undone and made a gentleman of? But I was willing to resign myself to my lot once more; all the more so that I had Miss Sandeman as my friend, and was to return home each evening.

"About a week after my arrival father made his appearance. He had come to carry out his part of the bargain—the educational part. Her face beaming in the morning light, she exclaimed as he entered—

"'Well, sir, here's a nice, crisp morning! Is Zucci to go to-day? He has scarcely got the glare of the foot-lights out of his eyes and the noise of the gallery out of his ears.'

"'*To-day*, Miss Sandeman—this day,' retorted father.

"''Tis well; Jesus is *in* all,' she replied, and made me ready.

"We left her. I was to return home at five in the evening. She dropped into my pocket a small parcel, saying, with a smile—

"'There's a little snap for you during the play-time—children grow best by having meat in due season.'

"She shook hands with my father and me, and followed us to the little gate, saying—

"'May God keep our feet from falling, our eyes from tears, and our souls from death: good-bye till evening.'

"She disappeared, and we proceeded. I saw in my father on this occasion what I seldom witnessed—reverence, genuine reverence. Old Mary's life and sayings always called it forth. After sundry advices as to conduct and faith in Mother Church we reached our destination. It was a large square building, surrounded by a high wall; the wall in front was surmounted by a railing. The visitor found access through a wicket in a huge iron gate, opened by a porter, a burly, red-faced little man, clad in a snuff-brown coat and clear buttons. After wending our way along a winding walk through a vast garden we ascended a flight of large steps, and were received by another porter, who, on learning our errand, asked us to sit down in the hall and disappeared. I was struck with the severe plainness of the furniture, and with two huge portraits on the wall: they were men tall in stature, thin in flesh; each wore a long red robe, and held a skull in one hand and a cross in the other. They looked as if they had just been drinking vinegar, and its sourness seemed to come through the skin of their face and out of their round jetty eyes, giving an acid feeling to the spectator's thoughts. Their hair, too, was coal-black and cut short, reminding me of that part of Jack Sheppard's person. On me they left a most disagreeable impression. Whilst scanning these two gentlemen in red we were summoned into the presence of a gentleman in black. After mounting some steps at the end of the hall we reached a nicely-carved door; on knocking, the porter opened it, and we stood in the presence of a remarkably thin intelligent-looking man. His features seemed all set on edge, the thinnest edges next the spectator; the ground-work of the countenance had to be traced like that of one of the relieved plans of Jerusalem; his brow was large, and beetled over a couple of grey eyes continually on the move; his head slightly inclined to the side; his voice was sweet and harsh by turns. When he spoke to you you felt fascinated, and listen you must. But one peculiarity of his face seemed to modify the expression of all its other features. When conversing with you you felt his lips were at your service, but his eyes were discoursing with some one else—he seemed to be keeping in check another being, seen only by himself. Yes, sir, he was a double man—wise, cunning, and prompt. To me he was two volumes in one always. This man was the head of the institution; its spiritual adviser, ruler, and tyrant. Before this mighty man in black father and I stood hat in hand. After a few quiet pokes at my father on account of the past, and sundry questions about the present, and on his promising to be a more faithful son of the Church, I was admitted a day pupil of the institution. I will not fatigue you with many details about the life I led at the school: how much I learned there my present condition will best reveal. As to knowledge, it seemed, according to them, to have fled from the horrors of the outer world like a frightened pigeon within their walls, and sure, had that house fallen knowledge would have been buried in its ruins, and never again appeared upon earth, unless Mother Church, in the exercise of sovereign mercy, had condescended to raise it from the dead. From their teaching, from their conduct, that was the only conclusion I could come to. Just before leaving this part of my history, permit me to mention another singular impression their mode of teaching left on my mind concerning religion: in their hands it seemed like a creature with a great many heads. Here the blessed Jesus appeared as a head; there it was Peter; yonder it was Mary; or, like the bits of glass in a kaleidoscope, it would fall into any shape you liked. Yes, sir; Jesus, the Saviour and God of believers, appears lost in a crowd of saints in their creed. Nay, once I was forced to say in my soul—I hope I was not too profane—in the gospel as taught by the Church of Rome Jesus is as difficult to find as a 'needle hid in a bottle of hay.' Another thing struck me very much in their system. Certain kinds of food, good and safe all the days of the week, on Friday became exceedingly dangerous. I was taught this lesson very impressively. The first Friday I spent in school, at the dinner hour, as the other pupils undid their little parcels of lunch; so did I. Some were eating bread and cheese; a few were rejoicing over the tail of a fish; others, with faces as long as the strings of their tops, were dining on simple bread and butter. I was overflowing with joy and gratitude over a nicely-prepared sandwich from the pure hands of holy Mary Sandeman. All at once a sharp little fellow sitting next to me started to his feet, and, raising his hands on high, exclaimed—

"'Zuccani! you sinner! eating beef on Friday! Master! master! Zucci! Zucci! Beef!! beef!!'

"The energy of his speech made his face bend downwards towards me. Not thinking that his gesture was meant to send his words into my soul, but was intended as an open attack upon my sandwich, in a moment I sprang past him, clearing in the same bound a number of forms. I retreated into the playground, and was making for the garden, followed by all the young 'Saint Fridays' of the school, headed by the master. Woes on me and my poor sandwich in that awful hour! We were hurled in the mud together! Two youths were ordered to lead me to the chapel; the others assembled around one of the pupils, bearing over his head my poor sandwich, all eyeing it as an unholy thing; but in their dinner-lists they set it down as something of a very different kind. Suffice it to say, the battle of the sandwich cost me some extra lessons, a season of excommunication, a solemn lecture on self-denial, and the loss of my lunch. One thing I did gain by this battle, and which none could take from me—a glimpse of the ridiculous side of Rome's penances. Every exhortation on this head appeared to me after this as a joke—as something from the leaves of *Punch*. One other reminiscence of this part of my story, and I have done with it for ever—the preparation of the youths for confessional. Among the pupils it is considered the grand step to holiness, pardon, and saintship. See that row of fine fellows, some of them the soul of all the sport in the playground? I am sure there is one sitting there among the candidates supposed to be, nay, called Old Father Fun, turned into a boy. How sad his merry soul looks to-day! Sleep and he have not met this week; ay, the story runs—light has been seen in his room all the hours of the night for a week; yea, even it is whispered, laughing Joe has washed out with tears all the merry marks in his happy face. 'What is the confessional?' I asked. Something very strange, it must be, I thought, to make Joe and these five others hang their heads like wheat-stems beaten with wind and rain. How kindly and tenderly all the teachers speak to them! Why did one of the five say to me the other day, 'Zucci, would you not like to be one of us—to be holy, to become a saint?' The awful day arrived: the separated ones were marched up, one by one, to a private door, through which Father Pennant, the man with coal-black hair, grey eyes, and edgy features had passed a little while before. All the pupils that day were still; the hum of school had died away; and, as if an execution on the quiet was being performed behind that private door, each head hung low, all seemed afraid to breathe, and every eye fell on that door, each apparently eager to get the first glimpse of the mangled remains of the first victim of some infernal mystery. I sat silent; I, too, was breathless. Memories of the unpacking-room tied my tongue and squeezed my lungs. The first one returned. The grey eyes, edgy features, and double tongue had done their work. It's poor Joe. Dear little fellow, what a cowed, crushed thing now; thoroughly thrashed; the very spirit sucked out of him! 'He'll never laugh again,' I said; 'he'll weep to the end of his days!' Poor Joey! I'll ever remember thee by thy jokes, and loud, loud laughter. Nay; priest nor devil will never unmake what God hath made; they may mar it, but destroy it they never can. Such were my reflections as I saw the frightened little ones led one by one from the hand of the destroyer with the grey eyes to a dark corner of the school, to finish in quiet meditation the rest of the mysterious work. All over, the holy father leads the man-made saints before the assembled school; an address on the mystery is delivered. The young saints are congratulated on their elevation. All are earnestly invited to follow their example; and the sanctified ones are led forth amid chants and hymns from their less holy companions to their dormitories and a good cup of tea. I returned home, sadly musing what these things could mean. Dear Mary Sandeman in one hour drove the grim meditation from my soul by a few verses from the dear old Bible. Ah, sir! the saints made by the Most High, upheld by the glorious Spirit, and washed by the blood of the covenant, stand longest; for when summer days were fine the faces of the five saints shortened, and dear St. Joe grew shorter in the face every day, and, like snow-flakes in the river, the five melted away among the common herd, and were only known from the others when the confessional-day came round by being less easy in their consciences and more hypocritical in their conduct. I, too, have passed through the fire, and remained as hard in my heart and as wicked in my life as ever. Well do I remember that sombre room, when only two sinners were present—one on the floor on his knees; the other, the bigger of the two, in a box, suggesting, by his cunning queries, sins, the existence of which, but for that infernal institution of the Romish Church, would have been long hidden from the young mind. Finally, sir, for I want to escape from this part of my story, one thing more I learned concerning Popery; its teaching never touches the heart; it hacks and hews the poor flesh, and on close inspection turns out an attempt to make clean the stream without *once* touching the fountain. Its poor victims are like boys on a slide—except God say No, they must go to the end of it, because of the pressure behind and the dark influences all around. But, sir, the hour of my redemption was drawing nigh. My father's restless soul was once more on the move. 'Break up, break up,' was once more the cry, and orders to march were once more issued. How was I to leave old Mary Sandeman—her sweet home with its three silent hours (the name she gave to her three periods of prayer)? Am I to lose sight of that new world she had just opened up to me, with its Jacob's ladder, Daniel in his den, the three holy children in the fire, and its blessed One, with his eyes shining with love, his heart breathing out prayers for them that slew him, and pouring out his blood that we might be dressed in snowy coats when we go to the palace of the great King. Dear Mary Sandeman! my father had my body—you captured my heart; and very soon by your prayers your blessed One won my soul. Murray and Mother weaned my heart from man: men unconverted are tyrants—demons. Rome, thy Church taught me the art of deception; the existence of certain sins known only within thine own walls; and this from thee I also learned—that the sinner's heart is beyond all improvement through the flesh. But, Mary, from thee I've learned that true godliness is a thing of the heart—the workmanship of the Holy Ghost; not of the will of man, nor of the groans of the starved flesh. That peace the Spirit brings, that Saviour who can save to the uttermost, and both endeared to my heart by thy holy life, dear Mary, I've found and resolved to cling to till I die.

"I was removed from Mary's care almost as rapidly as I was removed from that of Murray; but not in anger—in tears and with breaking hearts we parted. But, sir, you'll spare me the rehearsal; it would open all my wounds afresh. The cause of my removal was a resolution on the part of my father and mother once more to take a house again. It was resolved and done. Father and I found employment at a large paper factory; mother found employment in her house-work. All for a season went on well. A few weeks only passed away before change, the curse of our lot, once more appeared. This time, however, it was a change from restlessness to repose, from the world to the fireside, from the day of life to the night of the grave. Father was struck by that disease of which he now lies dying, and several years are come and gone since then. I remained at the factory, and, along with my mother, have done all to keep our home comfortable. My poor father is fading away, and soon will disappear. Often have I sat watching him as the day wore away, his eyes faintly shining, his mind wandering, and his voice so reduced as to resemble an echo dying, dying away among the rocks. How earnestly have I longed to know to what spot his weary soul turns for rest! Often do I cry that the Lord would meet him by the way, and stretch out a finger of his wounded hand, that father's troubled soul might perch upon it like a tired dove. Often my own soul catches father's melancholy, and I find relief generally in a long and lonely walk. It was in one of these melancholy walks that the great event of my life took place. I had been sitting by father's bed one afternoon, when his features all of a sudden became unusually pale, his eyes half-closed, and his mind wild and wandering. I got so unutterably sad that mother wept to see us both. I seized the first opportunity of going out, and, while musing in what direction to go, a sudden temptation to visit the theatre was darted into my mind with such *force* that in a few moments I felt powerless in its grasp and as helpless, and with equal speed was I carried to the spot as is the feather on the wings of the wind. I ascended the steps, and found myself in the pit. I had scarcely sat down, when 'Fire! fire!' re-echoed over the whole house. Such a scene in the gallery! nothing but swearing, rushing, and tearing; except when occasionally above all was heard the prayers of the down-trodden for mercy. The pit emptied itself on the stage, and, strange to say, I found myself flying from death across those very boards where I commenced earning a living. Escaping by the stage door, I found myself in the street, weltering among a sea of human beings. I cleared my way, making for home, but in the terror of the moment I had turned south instead of west. That fire stopped my return to ruin, it was to me what the glowing sword of the angel should have been to Balaam. Under an awful sense of danger and wrath, I wandered along a narrow lane, shouting aloud, 'Mercy, Lord! O Lord, mercy this time!' Whilst almost mad with fear, and in the darkest part of the road, I heard the sound of music; it was a number of people singing a hymn. I staggered to the door, waited till they were engaged in prayer, and slipped down among the kneeling crowd. After prayer I sat down, hiding my face in my hands. A little bright-eyed man, his face all smiles, mounted a platform and gave out for his text for the evening these words: 'Escape for thy life'—Genesis xix. 17. I lifted up my head—stared all around. I felt as if a messenger from heaven was at my heels, crying—'Now, or never!' I could stand it no longer; I gave vent to my sorrow in a shriek of despair, and I screamed out—'Where? where?' Methought the flames were gathering around me. The little assembly started to its feet, and its remarkable little preacher came up to me and said—

"'Into the arms of the Lamb of God, brother—escape there.'

"I stared wildly into his face, and made no reply.

"'Come, give us your hand, and we'll run with you.

"I intuitively laid it into his, he kneeling and gently bringing me to my knees. He now prayed, all the others kneeling round us. Oh! that prayer had power, sir, as the preacher agonized with God for me! He wept—he mourned; and sore did he plead the merits of the blood of Christ for me; then he seemed all of a sudden to get a glimpse of my condition before God, and the value of my soul. O, sir, then, as if at his bidding, an awful sense of my sins, like a horror of great darkness, hung over my soul! I fainted. When returning to consciousness the little preacher was the first to greet my eyes. Smiling through his tears, and intently gazing on me, he said—

"'The blood of Jesus Christ his Son cleanseth us from all sin.'

"My soul seemed to pause in her struggle, and on tiptoe seemed to listen; backwards, forwards, and upwards it looked. These words were soft as the music of the lute on a lake in the silence of night. All my iniquities seemed to fall into that blood, and my soul became quiet, and found relief in tears of joy. A sense of the mercy of Jesus so filled my soul that I absolutely danced for joy, and began talking to the trees on the road side about his dear name. Thus, sir, chased by the devouring fire from the stage, I have been caught in the arms of Jesus, where I long to live while here, and to sing for ever hereafter. That night I passed from death unto life, and, through my adorable Lord, will live for evermore.

"I have now told you my simple story. I ask you, as a friend, to provide a field for me more suitable than those I've laboured in, if you can. If not, I can still say, 'My Lord Jesus does all things well: thy will be done.'"

The writer may add, that poor Footy died after several years' illness, trusting in Jesus. The duchess, his wife, is an active working woman; has been taken by the hand since his death and is doing well; and she also is looking unto Jesus. Poor Zuccani is a godly servant in a gentleman's family, and one day may prove to all men that he that sows in tears shall have a reaping-time of joy.

CPSIA information can be obtained
at www.ICGtesting.com
Printed in the USA
LVHW100523120522
718524LV00004B/241

9 783375 001100